# HOW TO LEAVE A COUNTRY

# How To Leave a Country

### A NOVEL BY CRIS MAZZA

COFFEE HOUSE PRESS :: MINNEAPOLIS :: 1992

Portions of this book first appeared in *Animal Acts* (Fiction Collective), *Cream City Review, Kansas Quarterly, Karamu* and *Lullwater Review.*

The publisher thanks Jerome Foundation; Minnesota State Arts Board; the National Endowment for the Arts, a federal agency; and Northwest Area Foundation for support of this project.

Coffee House Press books are available to bookstores through our primary distributor, Consortium Book Sales & Distribution Inc., 287 East Sixth Street, Suite 365, Saint Paul, Minnesota 55101. Our books are also available through all major library distributors and jobbers, and through most small press distributors, including Bookpeople, Bookslinger, Inland, and Small Press Distribution.

For personal orders, catalogs, or other information, write to:
COFFEE HOUSE PRESS
27 North Fourth Street, Suite 400, Minneapolis MN 55401

Library of Congress cataloging-in-publication data
Mazza, Cris.
    How to leave a country : a novel / by Cris Mazza.
       p. cm.
    ISBN 0-918273-96-x (pbk.) : $11.95
    I. Title.
PS3563.A988H68 1992
813'.54—dc20                                   92-4005
                                                    CIP

Then he ran home to see, to touch again
The Ivory image that his hands contrived. . . .
. . . Touched her again and felt . . .
The pulse-beat stirring where he moved his hands.

—Ovid, *Metamorphoses*

[She] knew that there never was a world for her
Except the one she sang and, singing, made.

—Wallace Stevens

*to Michael*

# I

## ANIMALS DON'T THINK ABOUT IT

*It isn't working very well anymore. She's starting to act like an amnesia victim — which she isn't.*

Sometimes it can be fun living with Phelan. Except when he wants her to paint something or remember anything from their extraordinary past.

Once she wrote a biography for herself when an obscure magazine discovered her paintings. "Being both born and raised, Ms. Katz now resides. The only one of her kind, she is in constant demand for numerous awards. She attends functions. Living with sculptor Phelan Barklay, her life remains."

She has the magazine — she must've written the portrait.

Lately she wonders: If perhaps she could somehow remember working on any of these paintings, would she actually like it? He enjoys them, while she can only dumbly stare at them or shake her head as he describes a painting that sold or one they gave away.

And they're starting to have the same conversation over and over.

"Tara, remember that time we — "

"I can't remember."

"But I've *told* you—"

"But the only past I remember is *yours,* and it's *nothing* like what you tell me! *Why?* How come I remember *your* past—stuff you've *never* told me?"

She doesn't see herself in what she can recall. She'd be easy to spot: as tall as Phelan and nearly as thin, her hair like a banner, usually tied in colored bows.

*All I can do is try to distract her . . . buy time . . . so I can figure out what to do.*

His chessboard is glossy dark and light wood. He lines the wooden pieces up at their starting positions. "Look here," he says. He sits flat with legs outstretched, surrounding the chessboard on three sides, pulls it close to his crotch. "I want to show you the game I played last night."

Tara squats at the open end of the chessboard, facing Phelan.

"See, the opening is from the book." He reads the moves from his score sheet, advancing pieces, knocking off a few pawns. "Then I left the book moves as soon as possible. So I took this variation. It's not in any book."

"But I thought the moves in your books were discovered by grandmasters."

"So?"

"Don't you think if you memorized and used them for the whole game, you'd always win?"

"But Tara, this is so beautiful. Just look at this, see, if he plays his knight to here, then I take, he takes, I take, he takes. I'm a piece down but look at my position. See what I could've done?"

"Why didn't you do that?"

"Well, he didn't play that knight move. Instead he played here." Holding a bishop between thumb and forefinger, he clicks it against a pawn, pushing the pawn aside, placing the bishop on the pawn's square; and deftly, at the same time, he picks the pawn off the board between his middle and ring fingers.

"So I take this one here, then he takes, I take, takes, take and check. Now, if he moves his king to get out of check, I can go here, he pushes here to defend, I go here, check and win his queen."

"Then why didn't you do it?"

"See, back here, he interposed his knight to escape the check, so I went here instead. Now at this point, I'm still wondering if I shouldn't have moved my queen instead; let's see, if I go here, he takes there, I take, he takes, nope — I lose a pawn. Maybe I should've put this bishop here. Then when he takes, I take, he takes, I take, and I've traded a pawn for a knight. But will my endgame be strong enough?"

He continues musing, continues thumping each particularly good move or silently sliding the pieces on their felt bottoms for weak or defensive moves, then sharply clacking the captures. "And this would be mate."

She's undressed and waiting. Pulling him close, she kisses him, drinking from his wet mouth.

They slide easily together, made for each other. All he can say is her name, thickly, he cries and her name is his breath, his voice rising to screams, but always her name. His long white back arches, face to the ceiling, he calls to her hoarsely over and over until it's all out and he sags against her neck, still sobbing her name.

"Phelan." She rubs his shoulder. He slides off her, opens his eyes and smiles. "You feel okay?" she asks.

"Great. My nuts ache. I feel great."

"Will it be that way for me too?"

"It's hard for me to imagine what it would be like for you."

She watches a tear scarcely moving on his face until it finds a dip, a hollow, and drops into his mouth. She presses her face against his, their eyelashes tangle, everything is blurry, his eye is a large murky puddle.

*I gave her everything I could imagine she could want or need. But there are some things I just don't know how to give her. I almost wish I didn't know. Because I can't do anything about it for her. And I don't know what to do for myself. What was I wanting? What did I get?*

She lies quietly looking around. They have many paintings on the walls with her mark in the corners. Phelan said she painted them. Sometimes a new one will show up and he'll say she hid it when she finished it, long ago, because she hated it.

He sits up to rub the cat who always seems to be purring or sleeping at the foot of the bed. The animal lifts its head, yawns, stretches. Phelan picks it up by its armpits and holds it in his lap.

Tara also sits up. "Why'd you neuter him?"

"For his own good."

"But isn't that why he's so lethargic?"

"I suppose, that's what I've heard."

"Poor beast." She touches him. "Doesn't know what's missing in his life, doesn't even know that something is missing. But what if he does . . ."

"He doesn't care. No fighting. No late-night yowling."

"It's more than that," she says. "You know what I wonder?"

Phelan looks at her — a quick glance — then looks down at the cat again.

"I wonder what he thinks about. Does he ever wonder why he's living here on rugs and sheets instead of wild in the hills where he belongs."

"I doubt it. He belongs here."

"No, I mean, does he even know what being a cat *means?* If he knew, he might not *want* to lie around here all day doing nothing."

The cat purrs and rubs his head against Phelan's knuckles. "He's happy, he's content, what else does he need to know?"

Tara lies down again. "You know, I haven't painted any-thing for a long time."

"I know."

"Maybe I never did."

"Come on, Tara . . . you'll get over it."

"Think so?"

The cat yawns again and thumps onto the carpeted floor.

"Anyway," Phelan says, "he couldn't live in the hills."

"Why not? Throw him out there and see."

"He'd be back. He needs comfort and attention."

"Lazy brat — doesn't even want to remember who he is. Lets someone else tell him what he needs."

"But he doesn't worry about it. It would be pretty hard to be as content and comfortable as he is if he worried about stuff like that. Besides, someone else isn't telling him; he has an instinct to crave what's best for himself."

"Doesn't everybody?"

*It's worse than I thought. I don't know how much longer I can distract her.*

After a while he gets up to clean the bed. He bundles the sheets into the laundry and takes out clean ones. None of their sheets are white. The pair he chooses have lions, tigers and leopards lying all over them. He makes the bed around and over Tara, pretending she's not there, feigning surprise to find such a large lump in the middle of his carefully spread sheets. Then she lies naked on the lions and tigers while he goes to his workbench.

"Tara, I just saw someone looking through the window."

"Impossible. This is the second story."

"Maybe he climbed the tree."

"Why would anyone want to look in here?"

He grins at her. She gets up and puts on a robe.

"Let's go out and find him," Phelan says.

"Why?"

"Come on!"

They dress quickly; Phelan doesn't bother with underwear. "Let's go." He holds her hand and rushes downstairs and out the door. It's a clear summer night with a lopsided moon. They walk soft-footed down the long driveway toward the old highway that's hardly used anymore. Both sides of the dirt road are thick with wild oats, buckwheat, semi-arid shrubs like sage and tumbleweeds, low trees, tall rubbery bushes that taste like licorice (Phelan cuts the stalks, peels them, and chews them for snacks), and a few taller trees: pepper and fig, like islands in the chaparral, left over from abandoned turn-of-the-century farms. Old equipment rusts beneath the waist-high vegetation.

Their house, which Phelan built, is probably much like the old farmhouses might've been, but modified: huge picture windows in the upper story and a glass-enclosed belfry with a telescope. There are just two rooms: a combined bedroom and study upstairs, a kitchen/living room downstairs; both floors large, square, uncluttered, without unnecessary furnishings. Phelan built the few tables and chairs they do have, also the bed.

Crickets and toads buzz. Their footsteps crunch softly in the sand. Sometimes the bushes rustle, rabbits run or sleeping birds nestle farther into darkness.

"There's no one out here," Tara says.

"There was," he says. "If all I wanted was to go for a walk, I wouldn't have to trick you." He stops and looks around. Tara moves close to his side, but as she does he suddenly drops to his knees and begins crawling into the bushes off the road.

"Phelan!" she calls.

"Come on, Tara, there's nobody around—let's play wild animals." He moves farther into the dark shrubs, so Tara also crawls on hands and knees into the bushes, but she doesn't follow Phelan. She can hear him rustling and breathing, but no more so than any other large animal stalking in the night.

So they creep around, growling, tossing pebbles — which rustle other bushes as decoys — circling each other until they meet, pounce and roll around ripping, snarling, flattening grass, crunching tumbleweeds, gathering burrs in their socks and shirts. Laughing, Tara is the first to gasp, "Help!"

Phelan stands and pulls her to her feet and they go home together and go to bed.

The room is dark; he is breathing softly. "Did you know you hold me like a stuffed bear when you sleep?" she asks.

But he is asleep.

She wakes once in the night, her arm thrown against his face, his lips pouting against her elbow. She moves her arm a little, but his mouth stays with her, clinging weakly like a tired anemone, weary of being fooled over and over by a finger.

He opens one laughing eye.

"A suckermouth," she says.

He smiles against her arm and sleeps again.

He is so familiar.

She touches the palm of his hand and his fingers close around hers.

"I can remember you being nine, Phelan, why can't I remember being nine myself?"

He has told her she's always been with him. There are no documents; she's had to take his word.

Turning away from him, her toes find virgin cold spots near the foot of the bed, sending whispering chills up her long legs. She settles onto her stomach, her arms beneath her, her hands going to sleep there, tingling numbness.

*I don't know when or how I first realized it can't work. I suppose it makes no difference now. It's not just her, it isn't just a relationship: a whole world will be terminated as soon as she starts to deliberately remember. But there's nothing I can do about it. Just let her do it.*

Tara reaches to the side of Phelan's head to trace the inside of his ear, exploring. Her fingers buzz with waking up. She covers his ear with her palm, holds his head, edges closer, touches each of his quivering eyelids with the tip of her tongue, kisses him there, feeling the fragile shape of his eye, sucking gently. She puts her forehead against his, breathing his breath.

*She says throw the cat out into the hills and see what would happen, but I already know — he would go find himself a new home and family. That's the admirable thing about the cat — doesn't depend on anyone else to love him more than he loves himself. He wouldn't sit out there waiting for someone to find him and take him home. And he wouldn't go back to being wild — he can't become what he was before he was mine, he has no previous life to resume.*

*I told her I'm going lion hunting. I'll be gone in the morning before she wakes. I don't even own a gun. I'm just going to go.*

# 2

## ISOLATED INCIDENTS

Mother, if they hadn't let you have me, would you have been sad?
Maybe. But I wouldn't have known about you.
Would you cry?
You don't cry forever.
Would you die?
I don't think so, son.

The agency said he'd adjusted well to his placement with the DiMartinos. They asked him if he would like to change his name. He wanted to know if that would make him really theirs, and they said no, nothing could do that. Besides, Father said, you don't belong to anyone but yourself, we just support you.

What does that mean, *support me,* said Phelan who was seven.

Help you grow up, said Mother.

Keep you alive, said Father.

He found an ad for a plant sale, Adopt-a-Plant, so Mother bought him a small fern which he kept on his window ledge and watered faithfully, but when the family went on vacation for a week, Mother put the plant pot out in the garden, and upon returning home he found the fern had not died.

Mother asked him what he would be when he grew up.
I want to keep things alive.
You want to be a doctor?
Maybe a doctor. I want to support something.
He wants a wife, Father said.

After cutting his hair, Mother held a hand mirror so he could see his head from the side and back in the big bathroom mirror. All he could see were towels hanging from the rack and part of the shower curtain. He reached for the mirror. Mother let go. But the mirror fell to the bathroom floor and chipped away part of the plastic frame. Mother said, Look what you've done!
    He found a chess set in Grandpa DiMartino's garage. All the DiMartino aunts and uncles were in the kitchen. Most of them were helping Grandpa cook.
    You add the salt after the oil, Pop, Father said.
    Don't tell me. If it wasn't for me, you wouldn't be here to argue with me.
    There were no cookbooks.
    What's this, Phelan asked. He held the board under his arm, the box of pieces in one hand. His other hand held a white pawn between thumb and forefinger.
    You never played chess, did you, Pop?
    I tried to sell it.
    An aunt asked, Ready for the onions?
    I need the celery first.
    Has someone grated the cheese yet?
    There must be things in that garage no one's seen for thirty years.
    The water's boiling.
    Don't get in the way, son.

The DiMartino cousins were all watching television in Grandpa's front room.

Phelan played with the chessmen on the rug.

# 3

## WORKING AT HOME

Phelan, I don't know if I ever thanked you for trying to help me that time. Remember, it was one of those days that you noticed I wasn't working, probably because I whined, "I'm bored," or "I have nothing to do," while you pinched and poked a figure of clay on your workbench. "How about painting," you said. You pushed a very deep navel into the figure you were shaping, although it was quite a skinny body. "People would stand in line to have your talent," you said, then you told me that story of yours which, you say, represents the intrigue of painting: that one about some primal artist somewhere who was the first to mix blue and yellow, tentatively dipping a trembling brush into the new stuff then gazing at the green which dripped from the bristles.

I told you I never said I didn't *want* to paint.

You lifted the clay figure's arms — long thin arms, twice as long as the body; it reached for you as though wanting to embrace you.

Then you said you would help me. You explained while you dressed me in a smock and tied it in back and set up the paints and easel for me: you would tell me stories which would give me ideas for painting.

"Of course it'll work," you said. "Look around, all these paintings were inspired by stories I've told you. I'll bet I could even tell you the same stories and you would find something else in them to paint, some new perspective or image."

I hugged you and you patted my rump, but I don't think I said thank-you then; I was in too much of a hurry to start. You handed me a paintbrush and my heart raced. It was a brand new paintbrush.

# 4

## THE ULTIMATE EMBRACE

As long as he's not here this morning, I don't need to get up and try to do anything. I may as well lie around like the cat, the way I do when he goes to weekend chess tournaments.

Sometimes after a tournament Phelan will want to show me a chess game which he lost. It's a different Phelan who shows me the game at home — different from the Phelan who played it in the first place. He always says he learns when he loses; if he wins he doesn't learn as much. But usually I'm not watching the Phelan who is showing the game to me, and I hardly notice what he says he learned. I am always thinking of the Phelan who, a few hours before, had to sit there losing. I know he didn't *try* to lose just so he would learn something. He probably bent his head farther over the chessboard, sweated and itched and squirmed in his chair, losing. And I can't change it so he won't lose — he's got the losing moves written on his score sheet.

He does keep all his games written down somewhere, all the moves numbered, although we have no photographs, no yearbooks, no boxes of mementos, no letters or cards pasted into scrapbooks. But I can remember him without fondling souvenirs.

He had a paper route and used the money to enter tournaments, also saving enough by the time he was sixteen to buy a lifetime membership in the United States Chess Federation. They gave him a certificate and he framed and hung it over his desk. I've never seen it around here, but I know he had it. He looked at it a lot, when he glanced up from the chess set on his desk, as he studied a position.

*I studied chess because I understood it. I don't know why they found that so hard to comprehend.*

When it was cold in his room, he could move his chess game anywhere in his stepparents' house, even into the living room, where he sat on the floor and folded his lanky body down to fit the world of the board.

He never asked his mother if he could go to tournaments. By the time he was in high school he would just leave a note on the refrigerator, telling her he'd gone for the weekend.

Sometimes he called Saturday night, and they said, we knew you were all right, nobody reported an accident.

Every year the big tournament was in the desert, in a small town shaded by nearby mountains, drawing players from all over the state. It's hard to remember one year from another — except the last time he went when a girl came to the big tournament. He'd only seen Gwen at smaller tournaments, and she'd never been paired with him before.

He knew she was fat and had braces and her skin wasn't healthy, and she wore pigtails on the sides of her head, but she'd smiled at him once in Los Angeles. They knew each other's names. He'd never played with someone who might talk to him during the game, as they bent together over the board. She wasn't a very good player, but she had dimples and her eyes made half-moons when she laughed.

But this dumpy little girl at the chess tournament doesn't look anything like me. Actually, Phelan and I don't have a single mirror on the walls, not even in the bathroom. Everything around here is handmade; maybe he couldn't make a mirror. Sometimes we comb each other's hair.

He chose a table and waited for Gwen. When men played together they usually said "good luck" to each other when they sat down, and they usually shook hands. But (he was thinking) perhaps with her he should say something else, maybe "This'll be a nice change of pace." After all, the character of the game was determined by the pairing. If the other guy was a stuffy by-the-book player, so was Phelan. He was staring at the board as though figuring out his next move, but the pieces were lined up at the beginning and he didn't yet have an opponent. His chess clock wasn't ticking. He adjusted all the pieces so they stood exactly in the center of their squares and the knights, the only ones with true faces, looked sharply left and right, toward the king and queen.

He watched Gwen sign in, find out who she was paired with, and look for him. She had to ask a few other players who were also waiting alone for opponents. They shook their heads shortly without words, without looking up. Then when she did find him she said, "Oh, it's you — I'm gonna get creamed." So he didn't say what he'd planned. He said, "I'll be gentle."

She leaned stubby, somewhat scaly elbows on the table, held her hair out of her face with one hand, exposing a few pimples on her forehead. After she made her moves, she hit her button on the clock with her whole fleshy palm. Phelan kept his hands under the table, in his lap. He made his moves quickly, so that five minutes into the game only thirty seconds were used on his clock. After each move, he pushed the time button with a single fingertip, then sat as before, carefully.

Twice she held her queen and pulled back, but Phelan never called touch move.

"I'm nervous, playing you," she said.

Phelan put a finger across his lips, then whispered, "Don't move your queen yet."

"I've touched it."

"Don't develop your queen so early."

She made a visor with her hands over her eyes, staring at the board, so he couldn't see her face. Finally she moved a bishop, looked up, her clock still ticking, then said, "How's this?"

Phelan smiled.

After her next move, she forgot to punch the clock to stop her time from running. Phelan pushed her button. "Oops," Gwen giggled into her hand.

"Time's short enough without giving it away," he said. "Another little trick is, when you take a piece, don't put the piece down before you hit the button—punch the button with the piece you just took from the board."

"Oh. That's good."

These were the only whispers in the room full of clicking chess clocks.

"I wish we could play without clocks," she said.

"Time adds a new strategy. Some people maneuver the clock as much as they do the board—to put their opponent in time pressure. A win's a win. I've seen guys a rook down win on time. Aren't you going to let that bishop get into the game? He looks lonely."

"Okay." She almost forgot to stop her time again after her move, then shook the whole table when she batted at the clock. She sighed, "Yeah, I hate the clock. There are two things I don't like about the game, and I think they're related . . . somehow."

He moved a pawn, let a few seconds tick away, then stopped his time and started hers. "What are they?"

"You know," she said, "as it is, the game is never played to its ultimate goal—every other piece can get knocked off except the king." She held a knight, Phelan cleared his throat, she let go. "Anyway," she continued, "all you're allowed to do is give him nowhere to go, nowhere to turn, corner him, trap him, but then the game ends before the obvious culmination." She touched the knight again, picked it up and held it dangling over

17

the board. "And then this time thing — it keeps you from even getting that far. Somebody wins when no one's been mated. It doesn't make sense. We're supposed to be trying to kill each other's kings, but we're not allowed to actually do it. So, what — we just don't bother to try?" The knight in her hand flew in a circle above the board. "I don't remember where this was."

Phelan pointed to a square, Gwen replaced the knight. "Technically, you do have to move it now," he said.

"Oh, I know." She moved the knight. "So, anyway, that's always bugged me — even if we did play to mate, the game would be officially over before the king is actually taken by another piece — before he's killed."

"Maybe checkmate isn't death." He made a move and touched the button.

"So, okay, even if it isn't death, at least the high and mighty king would be captured, no longer free, a *prisoner.*"

"But that's not the same as killing him. If you take that pawn you might actually be doing me a favor — I could take back and free up my bishop."

"Oh, okay," she said. "Anyway, he would still *lose.* That's all that matters."

"Not if they make him their sex slave." Phelan removed a hair from the board, smiling a little. "Maybe that's why the king doesn't run away very fast — only one square at a time — he *hopes* he'll be caught, he knows it won't be so bad."

"Since when is losing not so bad?"

"It depends on your definition of losing. Maybe all the other pieces are groupies and he's the ultimate idol who they're trying to catch so they can hold onto him and get close to him. That's what checkmate would be — that climactic embrace."

"But what about *us?*"

"Huh?" He said it out loud, then looked around quickly. A few other players looked up at him, then resumed their positions over their own games.

"I mean," she said, "if it's *not* bad to get caught, why do we *win* if we *don't* get caught?"

"Well, it's a race — we want *our* groupies to rub up against the other king first. Here they all come, screaming across the board to catch their idol!"

"You're funny. You're teasing me, aren't you."

"Am I? You'd better make your move. I'm sorry — we've been talking while your time is running."

"That's okay." She bit her knuckle, looking at the board.

"No, let's move it back," he said. "Say, five minutes?"

"We didn't talk that long."

"That's okay."

A cat came into the tournament hall. He wandered under the tables, rubbing on the legs of people and chairs alike. Phelan put his hand under the table, wiggling his fingers until he caught the cat's eyes. The animal came to investigate. Phelan patted his lap. The cat crouched and leaped, landing on Phelan's legs, settling down instantly, facing the table, his eyes level with the board, but closed.

"Wait," Phelan said as Gwen began to move a rook. "I'm attacking your knight, you'd better do something about it."

She began to look up after each move, and Phelan would smile or nod or shake his head. The cat purred.

"Can I move my queen yet?" she said.

"Sure. You've got a great position."

"I don't know about that. . . ." She stretched her legs and touched him under the table with her foot. "Sorry."

He hooked his ankles around the front legs of his chair. Reaching for a piece, he brushed her hand. "Sorry, I thought it was my move, isn't it?"

"I don't know." She giggled softly.

They checked their score sheets and began again.

"I don't know. . . ." Phelan said.

"What?"

"I don't think I'm gonna get out of this . . . unless maybe . . . no, heck, I shouldn't've. . . . Darn, look at this. . . ."

"Huh?"

"Mate in three. All my moves are forced." He stopped the clock and stood up, holding the cat. "Good game." He offered her a handshake and she accepted, knocking over her king as she reached across the table.

"See you," she said. By the time he'd put the cat back onto the floor she was already gone.

*I never play chess with Tara. She told me she already knows what the outcome would be, so what's the point of playing through. There was also no point in arguing.*

In the second game, Phelan played an older guy who removed captured pieces by pushing them aside first, then slowly picking them off the board like dirt. I'm surprised he didn't just flick them back at Phelan as though they were peanut shells he'd dropped there.

In the middle game — after a particularly daring move, and with his opponent's time running — Phelan stood up and stretched. He had a stiff neck or the beginning of a headache. He went to the restroom, then stood at the mirror for a moment with his eyes shut. He ran water over his fingertips.

The restroom wasn't in the main tournament hall. There was a small lounge, deserted during play, unlit and cool. Phelan came out of the restroom and saw Gwen lying on a couch in the lounge. She was large and shapeless, like two blobs of ice cream side-by-side, melting together. He didn't look long, but he also didn't move. Then she saw him and sat up.

"Finished?" she asked.

"No, just taking a break. You?"

"I lost this time — as easily as I won our game."

He nodded. "I probably should get back. . . ."

"Yes." She stretched. The buttons of her blouse pulled tight in the buttonholes. "I meant to tell you, I really shouldn't've beat you."

"That's okay."

"No, I mean . . . should I thank you? I mean, I wouldn't have won, you know. . . ."

"Somebody has to win," he said slowly. "Unless . . . too bad we didn't draw."

"That would've been okay with me," she smiled. "You should've asked, 'cause, you know, *I* didn't win the game—you know that. *You* won, but you won with my pieces. I didn't have a choice. That's kind of funny—I was actually forced into winning!"

He sat down beside her.

While playing most chess games, Phelan thinks pretty extensively before making any move. Reading through the game afterward is much quicker, no long stretches of ticking silence. Yet once when I was replaying one of his games, he caught me. He watched me for a moment then said, "What are you learning by just making moves? You should study each position." I said I didn't feel like learning and leveled all the pieces off the board.

"And now, you're probably out of contention for today," Gwen said.

"Maybe." He looked at his knees.

"It doesn't seem right—I still say *you* won our game."

As he looked at his legs, her hand crept onto his thigh. "Forget it," he said. "I mean, don't worry about it. I've lost tournaments before." He watched her hand moving on his leg, back and forth.

"Have you?" she said, and she began moving her hand nearer his crotch.

"Well, sure," he said.

She squeezed his leg, her hand now far up his thigh. He wondered if she knew that two of her fingers were very near his penis, where it lay coiled in his pants. He shifted, so she was touching it. She pressed slightly with her fingers. "Of course—every time you play a game with yourself, one of you has to lose. I just wonder how you ever manage to raise your rating that way."

Phelan looked away, looked around, looked down at her hand, now all the way in his lap, cupped over his crotch. "I'm almost an expert," he blurted. She tightened her hand; his face was getting hot.

"I mean," he said, "if I can put together some match wins this year, my rating will make it to the expert level."

"You aren't an expert yet?"

"Class A."

She kneaded him slowly — so slowly her movements could barely be seen, although he continued to stare down at her hand. His pants were bulging. Inside, it was bound and twisted. He wanted to adjust himself, to reach in his pants and bring it up to where it was trying to go. It was bent to one side, held down by his underwear. It needed more room, but she pressed down against it, and that hurt. His leg muscles leaped, his hips jerked. Gwen smiled.

"So," she said, "that game I supposedly won put off your expert title a little longer. Too bad. I hope it wasn't your only goal in life."

His pants were pinching him and he twitched again as she pressed down. Gwen slid off the couch, plopped on the floor beside his feet, releasing the pressure on his crotch, and he released the breath he'd been holding. She put her chin on his thigh. They stared at each other. He bit his lower lip. He felt her hand return to his groin, this time to his zipper.

He said, "Wait." His hand held her wrist.

She stood up. "What's the matter — don't you want to?" Her eyebrows high, her voice like a child's, only her eyes were laughing.

He stood and faced her.

"Attaboy!" She giggled as she spoke. She took his hand and started to lead him to the restroom door.

He stopped, pulling his hand away. "The *men's* room?"

"Come on!"

He kept looking at her until she turned and went into the restroom, then he followed.

He sat on the only toilet, in the only stall. But it didn't have a door. Phelan remained fully clothed. She was kneeling, her heels pushing into her huge ass. At first he held her shoulders like handles. Her chest pressed into his knees. She unzipped him and fished around in his fly, obviously confused by his underwear. She dug into his pants, caught him, her fingernails were square-edged and rough. His mouth opened but the scream was silent.

Then he didn't look down. He was out of his pants — at least he was free of the binding pressure. But he didn't need to look to see that she held onto it like a plunger, with both fists, pumping up and down vigorously. Awful sound began to come softly from his throat, and she looked up, smiling. He shook his head, mouth open, his fingers dug into her shirt, balling the material in his fists.

"Okay, if you say so," she said. She stopped long enough to pull her arms out of her shirt. Unhooked her bra and flipped it away also. He shut his eyes but could feel what she was doing. She lifted her breasts and put them on his legs, one on each knee. They didn't feel like arms or hands or elbows on his lap. He opened his eyes and looked: two blobs. He groaned, then she grasped him again and he jumped, jiggling the load on his knees. She worked at him again while he cupped both hands over his mouth, staring: the color on her tips was as large as baseballs, and there were really no nipples, not at all pert and pointy (like mine). They were round and dumbly staring at him.

Her hands were two fists, one on top of the other. When she finally stopped pushing up and down, she began to twist, rotating her fists around him in opposite directions. It felt like she was rubbing the skin off and all he'd have left would be a polished skinny stick. She laughed as his trembling legs made

23

her blobs quiver. "I didn't think men liked jiggle anymore," she said. "And yet, I'm much better at it than I am at chess, aren't I?" He shook his head, then grabbed his hair, then clutched the toilet seat, then cupped his face in both hands. He finally managed to gasp. "Wait, slow down a sec," and he toppled sideways, hit his head against the side of the stall and stayed leaning there, holding with both hands onto the toilet paper roll.

He was still very hard. She released him and blew on her reddened palms. "Whew — you don't get off easy, do you?"

"Easy?"

She straightened her back, lifting her breasts from his legs. They pointed to the floor. She stretched, arching backward until she managed to make her breasts look like they didn't droop too much. Phelan watched dully. He remained hard. He wondered why.

Gwen stood and peeked outside the edge of the stall, hiding her chest unsuccessfully with one hand. Turning back toward Phelan, she began to unbuckle her own jeans. "I think we have time — "

"Wait!" he sat up. "Wait, I forgot!" He stuffed himself back into his underwear and pushed past Gwen. She was wiggling her hips, trying to get her jeans down over her ass. "My game!" He tried to run, but his knees were rubber, and he collapsed just outside the stall, holding onto the urinals. His legs kept buckling, his head almost in the trough. He felt sick, turned and sat on the edge of the porcelain, swallowed, his stomach flopped.

"Still here?" Gwen came from the stall, fully dressed.

"I'm going."

She called "Good luck" as he left the restroom. She wasn't coming out behind him.

He could see even before getting to his table, his opponent was putting the pieces into a bag. He could also see the result of the game already written on the wall chart. The older guy looked up at Phelan. "It's over. Your time ran out." The guy dropped a king into the bag, like playing the clothespin-into-the-milk-bottle game, then added, "Thought you'd died."

Phelan sat, looked at his lap, then very slowly zipped up his pants.

# 5

## LION HUNTING

The trees are as dark as the sky, or darker: deep black places overhead where the stars are blotted out, barely moving, whispering. It looks as if the stars are the ones swaying, in and out among the leaves. The pre-dawn is screaming with crickets and toads. Phelan stands on the doorstep.

*I honestly didn't think there'd be a time limit to Tara and me, but there is, and it's short—and I don't have any more ideas to change anything before the time's up. In chess it's the worst way to lose. You could be playing a strong game, have a winning combination, even be ready for checkmate, but if your flag falls before you win . . . you lose. I don't know where I'm going. Yes I do. I just don't know why.*

It is summer, but this is the coldest hour of the day. He's wearing shorts and a sweatshirt and tennis shoes with socks. Normally he doesn't wear socks, but the grass and weeds in the hills are dry and scratchy this time of year.

He cuts across a field, staying on a narrow path which hasn't been used for a long time. He watches his feet. If the path had been used regularly and recently, he could feel safer, because he could be sure wasps wouldn't have built nests anywhere along it. But now he has to be careful to put his feet down only where the ground is hard and flat, not on loose rocks or old boards.

*It's like sitting in the living room then getting up, with a purpose, to go into another room in the house to get something. But when you get there you've forgotten what you're looking for. You stand and stare at everything, then go back to the living room and retrace your steps, but you still don't remember. And if you're with someone — a friend perhaps, or your mother — they might say, If you can't remember it, then it must not have been very important.*

The hills are not far, rounded and not very high, the grasses and bushes the same as in the fields. The trail is slightly uphill now, and grown over. Nothing grows on the trail, but the bushes lean over it and brush his legs, leaving their seeds in his socks so he can transport them to new places to grow. Round ones with thorns coming out in every direction, or long ones with a single barb. In the spring he could've pinched a stalk of wild oats between thumb and forefinger and zipped all the green kernels off in a single motion, but now after they've turned brown, the stalks are tough and dry and the kernels open and papery, and if he tried to strip a stalk he would cut his hand.

Now beside the trail there's a formation of boulders like an island in the grass. He leaps from the trail to the nearest rock, mindful always that he doesn't put his foot down in the weeds where he can't see the ground. He jumps to the highest rock, only slightly higher than the others, and certainly not the highest point in the hills, but it's the first place to stop and look around. He stands and circles slowly, one hand held like a visor at his forehead. But it's still pre-dawn, and there's no sun to shield from his eyes.

The eastern hills have a lighter sky behind them, so they appear to be the darkest land. Only a very few tiny window lights from ranch houses on the horizon of the eastern hills, and to the west, many more stars than can be seen in a city

27

night-sky. But dawn will accelerate now, and the next time he stops to look, the stars will have faded.

The western hills are where people live, where water was first piped in, so they're now covered with green lawns and gardens. Olive trees were imported in the 1920s for an orchard several miles square, so now each house has at least two of the old trees in its yard. It was a much longer walk, when he lived there with his stepparents, to come over to these drier, barren, undeveloped hills. Now, he can get to this first lookout point within five minutes. He glances at his watch, but it isn't on his arm. He left it behind unwound.

*Or it's also like going treasure hunting when you're too old to believe anymore that pirates came inland or robbers had a fort here and hid their money somewhere in the hills, but you go out poking around like you used to, and you may even bring a shovel, because it was part of the outfit, like the safari hat that's getting tight, but you don't do any digging, not even for arrowheads because you learned in school that the only Indians around here were scavengers — there was never much water and no real game to hunt.*

*Once after it rained I came out and made paw prints with my palm and fingers because I'd told my friends there were lions in the hills.*

# 6

## WORKING AT HOME

Luckily it was a day you didn't have to do pottery. You may think I haven't noticed, Phelan, but when money is tight you move to the wheel and churn out one- or two-hundred bowls or urns, drip glaze on them ("artistically," you grin, slapping color onto the pots), then cook them and sell them to a tourist shop in the park. You never talk much at the wheel; it's business. The day you tried to help me, however, was one when you didn't have to spin the wheel, so you were able to work on that abstract female figure.

"Another me, I suppose," I said.

"You think I'll quit after making you once?"

"Ha ha."

But then you told me I inspired you and that's what you were going to do in return for me, like you used to.

"You did?"

You pointed with a clay-coated hand. "That one there, it's straight from something I told you."

It was *Clam Bake,* a beach picnic at night, nothing distinct in the firelight, forms and shapes of people, the black-glossy ocean in the background, flat-black sky, grey sand with patches of darker shadows. And near the firelight: a chess-

board, drawn in the sand, with a game in progress, but no
players.

So there I stood with a new paintbrush. "Okay, let's try that
one again."

"Well, it was a big chess tournament, all the masters and
grandmasters were playing. The only tournament being
played anywhere. The last tournament left. I wanted to stay
forever. No boxed-in tournament hall, quiet and shuffly and
old guys coughing. They had fires up and down the beach, as
far as I could see both ways, bonfires, and the boards were set
up on low benches in rings around each fire. We sat in the sand.
And no clocks ticking — just some kind of invisible bug singing,
you know, the way at night it seems like the stars are making
the cricket sounds. And the fires popped and hissed. There
were fishing poles, and the players who'd finished their games
would fish, then wrap the perch in foil with onions and butter,
and put them in the fire. Between games we went on walks — "

"Who's *we?*" I asked you. "Was I there too?"

You hesitated, absorbed in making the figure's palm by
pressing a fingertip into her hand. "Well, yes, I guess you were.
It *was* you!"

Then you told me it really had happened and could've been
our honeymoon, except we aren't married. You pulled your
stool close to where I was standing and told me how there
wasn't a moon, so when we walked down by the water where
the sand was wet, everything around us was shiny-dark, and
we could just barely see the foam when the waves broke, the
white catching a little of the firelight. You held my hand.

I asked you, "What happened?"

"Why does something have to happen?" you said, but your
voice quickly softened again and you went on, telling me about
the shell I found, a big one, bright pink inside, which I gave to
you as a chess trophy, but you don't have it anymore because
you must've left it in the sand by accident when you played
your next game. You held both my hands and I could feel how

hot your skin was underneath the cool layer of clay. "Gives me chills to remember it," you said, and you pressed one of my hands in your crotch and held it there. I didn't mind.

"We stayed at one of the fires for a while," you said. "The chess pieces looked rosy on the boards in the firelight. Like they were alive. You got chilly and sat beside me while I played another game." And Phelan, you reached under my smock with your free hand and touched my skin with cool clay on your fingers that made me shiver.

"How can I explain!" you cried suddenly, leaping off your stool, catching me, and together we fell onto the floor, tangled in that flapping smock, while you rubbed yourself against me. The clay from your hands painted me, a brown tint. You didn't hurt me. Your mouth was against my arm and you said my name, you kept repeating my name for a while, you told all the parts of me who I am as your mouth moved from one place to another.

"And then," you said, panting, "the tide was coming in. Each wave closer, they would pour up over the dry sand and melt into it. Each wave wet a little more of the sand which was still warm from the day. We were burying our bare feet in the sand as we played, to keep our toes warm."

You were hard all over, Phelan: your muscles and stomach, your legs and knees, everything; but your movement against me was gentle. You weren't entering me, except your voice, telling me how the waves got rougher, coming faster, wetting the sand, melting the hills of footprints between the fire rings.

"Some of the boys on the beach-side of the fires were wet to the waist," you said. "Me too. I kept playing. Some of them shouted every time a wave came all the way to the edge of the fire, and boys all around me had their kings washed over, forcing resignation, and they burned their boards and pieces in the fires. Tara—" You groaned for a moment, your face down against my neck. Your cheek was wet. "They were jumping up and burning their games," you said. "The last chess games. I was afraid. The water was so deep. I called to you. Where were you? I was standing up too, holding my board out of the water, keeping the pieces in place. I had a mate-threat. I was in an aggressive position. All my pieces were active. They all burned their games and the flames rose into the night until the water spilled over the edges of the fire rings and hissed, washing the ashes away, and all the boys had left, Tara, but not me. My game was whole. The last chess game. And you brought me a towel and a sweatshirt. Tara . . ."

And you went back to pressing my name against my skin with your mouth, rubbing yourself against me, rubbing the clay onto me, on the surface, on the outside. The only specific feeling was the foam, white and warm on my belly, on my skin.

Then you calmed and covered me with the length of yourself and groaned, "I wanted to play forever that night."

When you rolled off me, I got up, straightened my smock, picked up the paintbrush from the floor where it had fallen, went to the easel. I stood there. But I couldn't even decide which color to dip the brush into. Blue, yellow, green, red, black, white, purple, orange, I can't even remember them all. I stared at them, then put the paintbrush down.

But Phelan, I'm still sure you only told that story once: *after* that first painting already existed with my mark in the corner.

And I'm positive, Phelan, you never brought me along when you played chess at the beach. I don't remember it.

# 7

## ISOLATED INCIDENTS

He decided that only the tournaments he played in would be official. Only those players at those tournaments (and those games for those players) would be counted.

He used notebooks, hidden in his bedroom (never brought with him to the tournaments). In the notebooks he kept records: he made entries for all the players in each tournament, adding results for those he already had on record, listing the new players and computing their ratings according to their game results at their first tournament.

He used a new rating system: four points for a won game, minus four for a loss, two for a draw. He ignored the ratings actually posted at each tournament—those numbers were based on many games he couldn't consider official, games he hadn't seen at tournaments he hadn't participated in. They couldn't count.

He took the game results home from each tournament and figured the standings his way. He was the only one who knew everyone's true ratings. He never told them. He never told the man who was at the top of his ratings notebook that he was actually the world champion.

With his friends in the chess club, of course, he had to pretend that he believed in the posted ratings. But he knew the only real chess was the games he played, and the games played around him, at tournaments on his schedule.

He spent too much time with a girl at a tournament and not only forgot to play his own game, but forgot also to record all the other results so he could later compute new ratings.

He decided that tournament couldn't be official, and it wouldn't be allowed into his notebooks.

But it had happened, the system buckled. The chess pieces could stand and stare and lose — all by themselves.

He put his notebooks away, into his good-work box from school where he kept his English papers, science experiment reports, biology notebooks.

In biology class they had tried to hatch chicks in an incubator. Phelan had come to school early to turn the eggs every day. He came in between classes to turn them also. He wasn't allowed to leave any class in the middle so he could go to the lab and turn the eggs, but sometimes he could ditch the basketball game during physical education. He would run all the way to the lab in his gym shorts, so if anyone asked or caught him, he could point out this was exercise too. Then he would turn the eggs carefully, a quarter-turn, and make sure there was enough water in the bottom of the incubator, for moist heat. And he rested, bent, hands on knees, panting and fogging the glass window of the incubator.

He was there the day some of the eggs cracked. He missed the end of the basketball game and didn't go to math class. No one could make him leave the incubator. He stayed after school. The eggs trembled. The birds inside had tiny picks on the tops of their beaks, for breaking out. The hatching eggs all had little holes where the chicks were breaking the shell with their little tools. Phelan could see the beaks chipping away at the holes in the eggs. Then they would rest, and he could see them panting, a part of the body pressed up against the hole, pink skin and wet feathers.

They started to rest longer. Breathing rapidly, then breathing slower. They trembled less.

Phelan picked up an egg and peeled the shell away, widening the hole, helping. He would have broken all the shell away from the bird, but large portions were stuck, fused to the bird's body. That one died.

The others died too, without making their holes any bigger. They stayed warm because of the heat lamp. They just stopped moving.

# 8

## LOVE STORIES

Although I do seem to remember his childhood instead of my own, I still can't push my recollection of Phelan back beyond certain points. But there's no specific starting line dividing blank blackness from technicolor sound movies. I've got some grainy, blurry, black-and-white images, unnumbered, undated, out of order. Father's old television always took a while to warm up but eventually produced a lucid picture with enough contrast and some kind of story. Red ants in the sandbox at the playground, eating peanuts at the zoo, damming up the gutter after a rainstorm, collecting snails, the musky smell of the bush where mourning cloak butterflies were easy to catch, running somewhere, going to a birthday party a week early, searching the garbage pails on the curb for a stuffed cat with plastic whiskers which had been removed from his arms the night before. The buckle on his belt broke one morning before school, so his mother put a rubber band around his waist. It was uphill all the way home from school, but he took a shortcut through the field beside dead-man's curve where there was the foundation of a burned-down house. He and his friend whose name I can't remember — maybe it was a girl — joined a crowd watching some dogs mating. The dogs were stuck together, tail to tail, almost finished, but they couldn't get apart yet. They kept looking around at everyone, then looking at each other, licking their lips and swallowing. The crowd grew a little more. Someone gave Phelan some purple grape bubblegum.

Someone said, "Which way would they run?"

At first the dogs only cowered under the volley of sticks, cans and rocks, ducking and flinching. Then they did start to move a few steps at a time, first one going forward and the other backward, then stopping short and reversing their direction. Neither dog made a sound.

Phelan didn't explain anything to anyone. His stepfather raised rabbits in the backyard. Phelan fed and bred them. He pretended they were an endangered species: he had the last known living adult rare albino New Zealand white rabbits. All his acquired knowledge had to be applied to the breeding project. The doe had to be transferred to the buck's cage. If it was the buck who was transferred, he would spend too much time sniffing the corners of her hutch where she had slept. But in his own cage his whole attention was directed to his mate. The water and food were removed also, leaving just the two of them, without distraction — except for the project coordinator, who took notes and timed the courtship. First the buck nibbled on the doe's ears. From tip to base, several times. She lay in a tense crouch, all four feet hidden, ears flat on her shoulders, but one at a time he lifted them in his mouth, making sure to get to the tender spot behind the ear at the base of the head where the hair was thin and the skin only faintly pink. When he mounted her, he could still reach her ears with his mouth, so he continued to soothe her in order to get her to voluntarily move her tail to one side so he could achieve penetration and impregnate her — of course, the project coordinator knew this was the reason rabbits have long ears. The buck was supposed to have two or three falls each time he bred, but the good buck had died and was replaced with one who screamed after one fall. (Luckily another of the rare pink-eyed animals had been located for the breeding project to save the species.) Phelan made note of the new vital evidence that the species did have vocal capability. The doe made no sound while giving birth — they shot out of her looking like naked rats without eyes — but the new buck cried when he fell, and sometimes the young rabbits cried during the slaughtering if Phelan didn't hand his father the hammer fast enough after the rabbit was hung by its back legs over the blood-bucket. Phelan's father always swore and the hunting dog in the kennel barked if there was a death-cry.

The rule was: if he was allowed to feed and breed them, and take the young rabbits out to play on the lawn, then he had to help slaughter them eight weeks after they were born. After so much experience with the same operation, Phelan was like a surgical nurse. His father never had to ask for each tool anymore. Slaughtering was done in silence except the grunt in his father's chest as he hit the rabbit behind the ears.

Phelan had his part organized and timed perfectly. Lined up on the top hutch, he had a covered pan for hearts and livers, another pan for kidneys and lungs (which the dog got later for his supper), then two sharpened knives and the sharpening stone, then the hammer. Hanging overhead were the frames to stretch the skins. On the ground he'd prepared a bucket of salt water for the dressed rabbits, still whole, and an empty bucket — set below the place where the rabbits would hang — for the blood, entrails and heads.

Then Father came with his rubber apron and Phelan tied on his own apron. As Father selected a rabbit from the hutch, holding it by the loose skin over its shoulders, Phelan opened the slipknots in the ropes hanging over the blood-bucket. Father continued holding the rabbit's skin with one hand, with the other he put the back feet into the open knots, and Phelan tightened the rope on the feet. Then Father could let go of the rabbit — except he kept his hand on the ears to keep the animal calm and relaxed — while Phelan quickly handed him the hammer. Father held the rabbit's ears down, exposing the back of its head and neck. The blow had to be clean — breaking the animal's neck instantly — or the rabbit would scream. Few rabbits ever struggled, hanging there upside down as Father held their ears, unless Phelan wasn't fast enough or the blow missed its mark. But as Father raised the hammer, Phelan turned away and poked his fingers through the wire of the buck's or doe's hutches, wondering how they felt about seeing and smelling what was happening. But he couldn't plug his ears because as soon as he heard the hammer hit and the bones crack, he had to be ready to take the hammer and hand Father a knife.

Phelan also knew how dogs mated because a few times Father had hired his hunting dog out for a stud.

He knew about cats too — that a tomcat's penis has a sharp hook on the end and he hurts the female as he pulls it out of her so that she turns around and scratches him and they fight.

The whole activity in the foundation of the burned-down house didn't take long at all. The two dogs finally ran away together, the crowd in pursuit, until the inevitable popping apart, then the bitch yelped and ran, tail between her legs. The crowd broke up a little, into twos, threes and fours. The male dog was frisking about with a stick in his mouth.

Phelan followed the bitch. He had to run and he felt the rubber band around his waist break as he began to breathe harder. He became one of the people who captures animals for the zoo — for a moment, because it helped him keep running. He thought he lost her when he had to slow down and was walking along a street where the houses were slightly lower than street-level, with hedges and fences along the sidewalk, so he couldn't see the yards. But he could look down each drive-

way as he passed, and finally there she was, lying in an empty
carport, in a cardboard box near a door to the house, between
the washing machine and a metal tool cabinet.

Phelan walked down the driveway, one hand extended as
though holding some food for her. She was licking herself
under her tail. As he got nearer, he saw the naked skin there
was shiny and wet and slightly inflamed. Her red tongue
passed over and over it.

She didn't even stop to snarl—bit first then ran around to the
back of the house. Her teeth hardly broke the skin on the back
of the hand which had been reaching to touch her. He kept his
thumb and index finger in a ring around his forearm all the way
home, as tight as he could get it. He'd learned first aid at
summer school a few years before. When he got to his
stepparents' house, he drank three glasses of water right away,
then came back to the kitchen every fifteen minutes for another
glass, to make sure he could still swallow and therefore didn't
have rabies. When Mother said he was getting underfoot, he
took his glass and started drinking bathroom water. He
washed his hand at least ten times.

At supper he told them a little bit about it—that the
Randall's dog was going to be a father soon; he'd seen him in
the burned-down house near dead-man's curve, but he
thought some kids brought him home so he wouldn't get lost.

"Are those the same kids who give you that purple gum
which I've asked you not to chew? Your father gets it all over
the bottom of his shoes and it's difficult to clean off."

"But I threw it into the trash can."

"After you clear the table you can go do your homework in
your room."

Sometimes when Phelan cleared the table he pretended he
was a servant in a big house, starving and unable to eat the food
he served and cleared away, but clever and discreet and able to
sneak huge mouthfuls of leftovers on his way from the dining
hall to the vast kitchen. If it was meat, his waning strength was
instantly restored.

As he was studying chess, he heard his mother talking to his father in the family room on the other side of his bedroom wall. She said she'd heard that the Randalls were thinking of bringing their dog back to the pound. "He was fine at first, Mary said, so small, so cute, but he just isn't cute anymore. He's huge. He barks. He licks and his tongue is enormous. She says he puts his huge paws on Timmy, her youngest. They used to take him on the beds when he was tiny, but now she said he gets onto the beds and tears the sheets with his gigantic claws."

Father's voice was lower and harder to hear, but it sounded like he said the neighborhood could do without any dog who's free to add to the population of mutts.

# 9

## WORKING AT HOME

Well, Phelan, at least you didn't give up. You got off the floor and cleaned up a little, straightened your clothes, mopped up the mess, sponged me off a little too. I didn't move; you took my shoulders and turned me away from the easel, where I stood staring at the colors, and cleaned me up.

"Come on," you coaxed me, "we're okay." I nodded, then brushed my hair and tied it back with new bows and washed my face with cool water and brought another stool over to the easel and sat there. I guess I was ready to try again.

"This is a good one," you said, bringing your stool over to the easel too. You sat next to me. "You have to remember first that there wasn't a circus in town. That's important. Because, you see, we found a midget. Well, he was a very short man, maybe three feet. Maybe I didn't find him either; he found us, or we found each other. We were at the lake in the park, feeding the ducks, and he came down the path and walked right up to us and said there was a boy stuck up on a telephone pole."

So, Phelan, you went through that story too: You and the small man went to where the boy was caught on the telephone pole, hanging on by one arm, swayed gently by the wind. You told the small man to hold you on his shoulders so you could reach the boy's ankle. When the boy let go of the telephone pole, you stepped down off the small man's shoulders to set the boy on the ground.

I hadn't picked up a brush yet, but you said that's okay, the story wasn't over. They put you on the news that night, you and the small man. Naturally you were pretty excited as you told me that five thousand people called the television station and tried to claim that the small man was their child and they'd lost him or given him up for adoption years before or he was kidnapped from his cradle, and they wanted their dear boy back. The small man laughed at them and said he was raised by tigers, but he was probably kidding, you said.

So you finished the story, Phelan. I was very cold and had a headache and stiff neck (from making an ugly grimace, you said, and not blinking often enough and not relaxing my neck or moving it enough). But you leaned close to me, with one arm around me, and picked up the brush, and Phelan, you chose a color. Green. Of course, green. The way I felt. You put the brush in my hand. Granted, I did lift my own arm and hold the brush near the canvas, but not very long. Long enough that a drop of green fell onto my smock where it covered my knee. I put the brush down and rubbed the spot with my fingertip. You put both arms around me — trying to stop my chills and warm me up — and sighed, but not sadly.

# 10

## LOVE STORIES

At least there's one wall in here which doesn't have an ugly painting—because of the picture window. With the curtains opened, birds bump their heads against the glass, not believing it's there, so Phelan likes the drapes closed. Besides, he doesn't want people to be able to see us.

He used to pretend that nobody was supposed to see him—he and another boy would play a game of spying on two littler kids, watching them from behind trees or hiding in bushes, making fierce animal noises to scare the kids into believing lions or tigers were stalking them. After he grew out of that game, he sometimes still played spy by himself. It was best when he could be a spy and at the same time play some other game with other boys, which supplied the necessary situational complexity to his spying: playing with the other kids was actually a clever disguise so no one would know he was really a spy.

This was a little after the time the bitch bit him. He had that same friend, and they did most of their playing in an empty lot where there was an old gnarled pepper tree. They would have wars with the bumblebee nests, which were built in rocks around the trunk of the tree. First, they'd throw dirt clods and stones, then run through the field, zigzagging, trying to lose the angry bees who chased them.

Across the street was another lot, but it had a house in it, set back off the road, without a lawn, just a field full of tall grass and tumbleweeds. There were a few old hedges which hadn't been trimmed for I don't know how long, nearly covering the front of the house. No window was accessible and the door was nearly blocked.

They were hiding in the weeds across the street. Police cars came and went. An ambulance had been there earlier. One policeman told his partner, "We're not supposed to let them out — exterminators will take care of it."

"She died, you know," Phelan's friend said.

"Who did?"

"The old bag."

After a pause, Phelan said, "I'm going in there!"

"Why? It stinks like crap."

But the other kid didn't know that Phelan was a spy in a foreign country, sent to free the other spies who'd been taken prisoner.

The weeds scratched his legs, spiderwebs broke against his knees. He watched where he put his feet down because he'd stepped on a wasp's nest once — screamed, but hadn't told his parents. (His stepfather kept beehives and never uttered a sound when the bees stung him.) His mother never noticed the welts all over his legs. She'd long since stopped giving him baths.

He kept one hand over his nose and mouth. It was summer and the air appeared to be rippling. He could hear flies buzzing. The warped porch boards didn't groan and he was able to slip into the house without even a single creak from the door hinges.

At least fifteen cats scattered from the first room, almost silently, and he hardly saw them — they were gone before his eyes had fully adjusted to the darkness.

For furniture the room had one chair with four wooden curving legs and clawed feet, but just a few long green threads hanging from the underside were all that remained of the fabric. The seat was a pile of stuffing, matted down, brown and caked with the same stuff which carpeted most of the floor, thinner in some areas, piled high in others, bona fide shit. One corner had a small hill of cat food cans, all opened, emptied, shiny with grease on the inside. A few of the cans were side-by-side on the floor, apparently purposely placed there. Something at first seemed to be moving on the trash pile, but it turned out to be a cat corpse coated with flies who were squirming their way past each other to get down to the skin. There were two doors leading to other rooms, where the animals were probably hiding, spying on him. And there was one closet door, pushed halfway open by a jumble of blankets which were frayed and soiled and spotted with feces. That was all there was in that room.

Phelan kicked the door shut. I don't exactly know what his plan was — just like I can't recall what he was doing that time he gouged his wrist with a big rusty hook and didn't tell his mother because he couldn't divulge his classified assignment.

He picked his way through the shit, his footfall silent, following the swarm of cats from room to room. He held his left shoulder with his right hand, pressing his nose into the crook of his arm, looking out over his elbow, batting flies with his free hand. He didn't say anything out loud — it was easier to maintain secrecy if no one else could hear his transmissions. The cats knew he was there — and they knew why. But they didn't want to leave. That did not surprise him because he already knew that anyone held prisoner for a length of time did not always behave rationally. He was jail warden for his father's chickens, but he changed his title to security guard when he found out they were terrified of freedom. He was careful when he fed them that he didn't hold the door of the coop open too long; but whenever one of them did escape, all it wanted to do was get back inside, and frantically ran around the coop until it found the door again. Of course, the more frantic it became, the more difficulty it had finding the door, especially with Phelan there, holding the door open for the loose chicken while kicking all the others away.

The other rooms were much the same as the first. Filth and stink and one or two more dead cats, hidden in paper bags or under rags. Phelan checked each for signs of life. He lifted an old dotted dress where he saw clawed feet protruding. The belly was split with maggots squirming in it. He dropped the dress.

Going through the house, he stopped in what was probably the kitchen, where rats — he presumed — were under the sink. He could hear them there. One cupboard was half broken away. Hiding all but his eyes with his hand over his face, Phelan bent close to see nursling felines packed together with their yellow-eyed mother, who hissed and moaned in her throat. He flinched as she struck at him, then she coiled again under the sink.

He finally stopped and squatted by the front door, waiting. He folded his arms across his knees, rested his chin on his wrist. The other spies remained silent and hidden, and he continued to squat there. After a while he tipped his head back against the door, blinked his eyes slowly and began to hum, faintly at first. He blended the tunes of nursery rhymes with folk melodies — the refrain of one became the verse of another — then patriotic songs, war songs he thought appropriate for his spy-comrades, and when he ran out of those, finally singing over and over the circular tune from the wind-up music box inside his lost stuffed animal. He never left them. The police found him in the morning when they came back, but even then he wouldn't leave. He stood and watched, everything blurred by his all-night eyes, as the exterminators caged and removed the animals.

# II

## LION HUNTING

Back onto the trail, he continues walking, still slightly uphill. It will stay only a gradual incline except the few places where, for a shortcut, the trail was plowed straight up the side of a hill. Those were the places where — in summer and fall — he used to slide downhill over the thick dry grass, riding on slabs of cardboard, over and over. The flatter the tall grass lay against the side of the hill, the faster he could slide, but there were sharp rocks and sticks and thorny bushes, and falling off the cardboard was treacherous. His legs would be covered with white scratches, so before going back to the house he would lick his hand and rub his legs, making the white lines melt back into his own color.

*I didn't necessarily always run off to the hills when I was in trouble or unhappy — but when I found myself alone, this was the only place where it didn't seem to matter. One way or another, I found something — to do or look at or bring back to my room or to hide out here somewhere, claiming whatever it was as mine.*

The next boulder formation is several yards off the path and has its own thin trail leading to it. From the main path, the thin trail disappears after a few steps — it can only be seen step by step as it is followed. It's a natural rabbit trail and never changes. The rock formation is in a small gully, so the tops of the boulders are level with the grasses, and they also can't be seen from the main path. It's called Rocky Flats. Phelan didn't name it, nor is there a sign, but everyone who knew about it knew its name. When he went down in the little gully, the straight sides of the boulders rose far over his head. At one time it was all one boulder, but it had cracked apart, and the cracks had widened until they had become narrow passageways through the formation. It had been a fort and also the place he'd brought a sick dog he'd found wandering around the streets near his stepparents' house. He'd stolen a hotdog from the refrigerator and lured the animal to follow him to the hills. Finally they'd gotten to Rocky Flats and Phelan gave the frankfurter to the dog. Afterward the dog turned around several times in the grass, flattening a circle just big enough so he could lie down. The unflattened grass stood up all around him, hiding him almost completely. Phelan had come back the next day with more food, but the dog was gone. Phelan sat in the dog's bed and the surrounding grass rose above his head too, and he ate the hotdogs and cookies he'd brought.

The gully no longer seems as deep and Rocky Flats is only as tall as he is. The passageways seem to be growing back together. He reaches in and picks up a brown beer bottle and throws it as far as he can, then listens for it to shatter, but he doesn't even hear it fall. It's darker down here. He glances around, but sees no glowing yellow eyes, hears no throaty panting.

*What do you expect to find? What did I ever find out here?*

His father had given him a BB gun and explicit instructions: Use it to shoot rats and ground squirrels—no snakes nor lizards—and cats if they come into the yard. He used to shoot at green plastic army men which he brought out to the hills and lost one by one. But the rats never came out or stood still long enough. He did find a rat carcass once, on the trail leading to

49

Rocky Flats. It was different every time he passed the carcass. First the eyes stopped glittering. He was waiting for it to become a skeleton, but it disappeared before it was picked clean, when it was still a dry skin stretched over the bones, but hollow, without maggots, only ants inside and out.

He climbs back up the side of the gully and sits on the top of Rocky Flats. Everything is much lighter. The sky, pausing between black and blue, is grey and there are no more stars.

*Why was it I never brought Tara out here? Dumb question — I didn't need to.*

The crickets have hesitated, then a brave one begins again, followed by the others, one by one.

*Nothing unusual, I always talked out loud — up here. Never when I was alone in my stepparents' house; they would've heard me.*

Standing on top of Rocky Flats, again he circles, his hand shielding his eyes from the sun that hasn't risen yet.

*Anyway, it seemed like I always found something — or so I thought. Is anything going to happen this time? I don't think so. What if I find nothing but the end of the trail or the far edge of the hills?*

# 12

## WORKING AT HOME

You were drowsy, and you stretched, smiling. The green paint dried on the bristles while you stood up for theatricals. You stood in the center of the room and asked me to turn around so I could see you.

It wasn't in California, you said. That was important. It was a panther-fighting syndicate. People bet on their favorite and paid to see the fight. You were appalled.

How you broke it up: You disguised yourself as one of the animals and refused to fight.

You acted it out for me. You wore only your underwear because you no longer had your panther costume. You sprawled, again stretching your comfortable feline body. I kneeled beside you and you rolled over to lay your head in my lap. I didn't turn back toward the canvas. I was holding the brush in one fist. With my thumb I smashed the dried bristles. The green paint flaked off.

# 13

## LOVE STORIES

He's never gone lion hunting before. I would remember if he had. I don't know what he thinks he'll come home with. Maybe there's a bobcat or two out there. There used to be foxes in the hills, but as far as anyone knows they're all gone, like the rattlesnakes. The snakes used to come into the chicken coop at his stepparents' house. He had to learn to pin their heads and pick them up, then throw them down the canyon. Once after he took a snake out—just a king snake—the rooster got mad and attacked Phelan's leg. Phelan hit the rooster on the side of the head with a long stick which he usually used to keep the hens away from the door. The chicken almost died—it flopped around, eyes closed, neck all twisted. Phelan caught him and stood him upright, held him until he could stand by himself. Both of them were bleeding. Phelan broke the stick and threw it into the canyon.

I don't know when this was, maybe high school. Some things are harder to remember even though he was older. I know he was planning to go to someplace called Humboldt and major in animal husbandry, so he needed a job in order to afford an out-of-town college. But I'm not sure when he changed his mind; I don't remember if he hit the chicken after or before he got his job at the animal shelter. Maybe even after he quit. Luckily every school has an art department, so he could stay at home and study that. As soon as he figured that out, he didn't need his job anymore.

Some parts of the animal shelter are impossible to remember. I don't recall any interview nor any training, nor who would've been the one to train him. But I can see him sweeping the corridors between the rows of kennels, then going into each cage to remove the offal and change the water, or hosing down the floor if the animal had been sick or the flies were bad. I remember the scalp-prickling sound of the shovel when he scraped up the crap and the echoing racket when one dog started barking and the rest had to join in.

I also know that his stepmother told him to be sure he used something before he left work every day so he wouldn't bring any fleas home. The only thing he could've used was the flea powder he put on the kittens when they were adopted. But he didn't use any on himself.

He volunteered to stay late on Friday and finish up.

There were four kitten kennels. At the end of a week, all the kittens moved up a cage, leaving the first one empty, just overnight, before it started to fill up with new arrivals. The cats in the last kennel were always a little larger than the other kittens, with louder voices. They were also mostly grey. Usually yellow, orange and calico got adopted before they made it to the last cage. The grey cats climbed the sides of the kennel, clinging to the wire, screamed in Phelan's ears and nicked the side of his head with their claws.

This is one of the only things I can remember him doing there. He emptied the last kitten kennel into a portable cage. He caught them one at a time. Their claws stuck to his clothes, so he had to detach each claw on all four feet separately before he could put the cat into the small cage.

There's a blank here—I don't remember where he took them. I don't think he did this enough times to allow me to recall every detail. In fact, I don't remember him doing it more than once. He took the first one he touched, pulled up the loose skin on its back with his thumb and forefinger and pushed the needle into that flap.

# 14

## WORKING AT HOME

In a moment, you pulled me down beside you on the floor, holding me the way you do in bed, while you sleep, your mouth behind my ear. "Think of this as artistic foreplay."

You said you would tell me one of your favorite memories, the time you had a place called Animal Oasis.

"A bestiality commune," I said. "Wow." You should've slapped me.

But you explained: it was a refuge, an abandoned barn or something, with stalls and a hayloft which was a little sunnier than the ground floor because some boards were missing from the roof. And it was huge, you said, room enough for all the cats and dogs you could bring there. "All day," you said, "the puppies could tumble together in the warm straw and the kittens could lie in the sun in the hayloft, luxuriate and sharpen their claws on the soft wood, stretch out side by side to lick each other's ears, playing together, holding onto each other and rolling back and forth, nipping each other's necks, until the game softened into sleep with one kitten curled around another."

Then you said the best part was when we were there with them.

I told you I was never there.

"Yes you were. I never saw you so happy, Tara. Glowing and ecstatic."

I told you I've never been ecstatic.

You continued to hold me, your mouth next to my ear. "I don't know what happened," you said, "but they were all poisoned." And you told me it didn't matter who or what; somehow the water must have become tainted, or some gas fumes came from somewhere. "I swear I don't know — it just happened."

The animals all slept, drugged, barely alive. You rushed from one to the other, prodding them, calling to them. They wouldn't wake. And they all rolled to their backs, bellies swelling, tongues protruding, legs stiff, eyes half open, glassy, dying, all of them.

"On top of everything else," you said, "the sun was so hot that it was drying them out. I couldn't figure out why it was so *hot.*"

"Maybe it was a forest fire," I said.

"Yes, yes!" you screamed in my ear. "There was an old bathtub in the yard — I filled it with fresh water and threw them in; they floated like ice, even the cats. I stayed there, kneeling beside the tub, just in case they rolled over and put their noses under."

Then bulldozers came, and helicopters hovering, and trucks and lots of men. They were digging and shouting at each other. Pounding nails. Running chain saws. Roaring engines. Cursing. Farting. Laughing. Belching. Dragging logs. Pushing piles of dirt. Shoveling. Rolling boulders. Pouring concrete. Emptying dump trucks. Filling dump trucks. They didn't see you. When the fire went past, they went away with it, making roads so they could keep up.

Then you told me how you fished the animals out of the water and brought them inside, arranged them on the straw, tucked their feet underneath them, laid their heads down, dried them with towels.

"They started to move in their sleep," you said, "burrowing close to each other in the straw, the stall full of their drowsy bodies." They were alive, and you said we took off our clothes and joined them.

Then we all slept together. "A deep and fearless sleep," you said, "sprawled out in the patch of sun, until it passed over and the shadows were cool." They rose, you said, ready to play outside in the late afternoon sun, and we made love. Your telling of it became more breathless, in my ear. Your voice quickened: "Tara—" Again. Your arms quivered. Your body tightened. Your breath in my ear sounded hysterical. I thought, again, again, again, again. You went on panting and trembling until, finally, your familiar last sigh. That's when I proceeded to weep and pound on your chest. Very melodramatic and disgusting. But you—you held me and patted me until I stopped, abruptly and dry-eyed. You looked at me with artistic scrutiny, then touched my face and smiled.

# 15

## ISOLATED INCIDENTS

A membership in the zoological society cost him only twenty-five dollars out of his summer savings. It allowed him free admission to the zoo for a year. He went almost every weekend.

He told Mother he had a date, so she let him pack enough sandwiches for two.

Why doesn't your girl fix the picnic?

She can't.

Phelan usually went to the children's zoo after lunch and tried to give a sandwich to a different goat every week.

He finished two drawings on every trip. Pencil sketches. Sometimes, but rarely, he shaded them with colored chalk. The pair of drawings were always of the same animal, a different animal every week, two points of view.

He showed them both to Mother when he returned home on Saturday evenings.

I did that one and this one is hers.

Why doesn't she take hers home?

She can't. They're a matched pair.

He had two elephants, two bears, two seals, two zebras, two spider monkeys, two foxes both asleep, two lions likewise.

There was a hospital at the zoo where they tended new baby animals whose mothers rejected them. Sometimes they took the babies away from the mothers regardless of how the mother felt about it, to be on the safe side with endangered species. The chimps and gorillas and orangutans were always raised in the hospital nursery. He watched a fawn grow up there. Also a litter of wild dogs. All the hospital rooms had large glass windows so the people visiting the zoo could see the baby animals. His favorite was the little black leopard who'd been mauled by her mother and rescued before she died, then operated on by zoological surgeons.

The little cat lay on her side, glossy black, her eyes pressed shut, a wide white bandage wrapped around her middle. One Saturday she opened her eyes and raised her head and looked back at Phelan through the window. That whole week he came every day after school, working a little every afternoon on a sketch of the black kitten and white bandage. She didn't open her eyes again, but in his sketch she lay with her head up and eyes open.

Mother asked if he was seeing his girl every afternoon this week.

He said yes.

A girl in his biology class looked at him through her fingerprinted glasses and asked him if he would escort her to the senior prom.

He said sorry, he had a girl who went to a different school, and he would probably go to her senior dance.

The little black leopard with the white bandage was named Tara. There was a sign saying so in the window of her hospital room.

Mother said she hoped to meet his girl soon.

On Friday he went back to the zoo to finish his sketch of the leopard.

She was gone.

He couldn't find her in any of the windows. Her name sign was gone too.

He asked a gardener raking leaves, but the gardener didn't know. He knocked on a door marked Zoo Personnel Only. Finally someone came to the door, frowning. The little cat died, the lady told him. The operation was a success but she died of complications afterward.

He hadn't finished the sketch.

He lay dozing in bed a long time Saturday morning.

Are you going to the zoo with your girl today, Mother asked.

No. I'm going alone.

He sat and fed pigeons outside the monkey houses.

When Father's parents came for a long visit, Phelan took Grandpa to the zoo.

Grandpa had been in the hospital, and his children had decided he and Nana couldn't live alone anymore. They were selling Grandpa's house. Grandpa wasn't thrilled about it. He yelled at Phelan's stepfather in Italian.

Mother told Phelan not to let Grandpa walk too much at the zoo.

Get him a wheelchair, son.

Father yelled at Grandpa for weeding the garden and sweeping the driveway.

Grandpa cursed in Italian.

Phelan said he was going to work all summer and make enough money to take Grandpa on a trip back to Italy to see his hometown, which he'd left almost seventy years ago.

No, son, Father said. He likes to remember it the way it was. He thinks it hasn't changed. If he went back and saw it, it would break his heart.

So Phelan decided to save his money and take Grandpa somewhere else, someplace he'd never seen.

He asked Grandpa where he'd like to go, and Grandpa said, home.

# 16

## TEMPORARY WORK

Why should I force myself to struggle with what I don't remember very well when there are things he did that I can recall in complete detail? If I can hardly remember something, it makes it seem like he hardly did it. But when I start to remember another job he had — this one while in college, just a part-time thing, a few scheduled hours five days a week — it seems that's *all* he did. As though the whole three months was spent in that old folks' home, going back and forth in the halls, in and out of those rooms. The memory of it wants to claim he never did or thought about anything else — a two-hundred-hour shift.

It was an easy job to get. He was filing applications at all the shops in the business district — even the greasy spoon and the health food store, family-run operations which didn't hire extra employees. All he wanted was a routine job with a time clock so he could afford a studio apartment he'd moved into where he was going to be an artist in his spare time while he went to college. So Phelan went into the hospital lobby and filled out his forms in the sitting area. One painting hung on each pea-green wall, thick wooden frames, prints of flowers, still-life wine-and-cheese, a sunset over the beach. Vinyl chairs and plastic coffee tables which come in a kit, including the glass ashtrays and bouquets of straw flowers. The carpet was a darker green, not plush because the food and medicine carts had to be able to move across it, and because of germs, and because of spills — dark outlined stains where puddles of pureed food had spread. And no matter the amount of disinfectant in the housekeepers' buckets, everything always smelled faintly of urine. Sometimes not so faintly, then some old guy would shuffle by, or wheel himself past, unaware of the wetness on the front of his pants.

They didn't get many applicants who could work in the men's ward. It preserves some of the old fellows' dignity, the receptionist said, to have a few orderlies, when, after all, they're surrounded all day by nurses and nurse's aides and have little real privacy. "You know," she smiled, "if they have to be helped to the toilet, at least they don't want it to always be a woman there helping."

*The agency said the adoption went well and my adjustment was successful. That was thirteen years before. My family came complete with aunts, uncles, grandparents, reunions, Christmas and New Year's Eve parties, the biggest Father's and Mother's Day gatherings, piles of presents and tables of food, housefuls of conversation, lots of advice. No one was ever alone.*

His mother was pleased with the job. She said, "It's a good sort of job, for temporary work. Those people need someone. Certainly better than working in a gas station. I'd hate to have you come home smelling of gasoline."

"But I won't be coming home here anyway."

"Surely you'll visit."

"I won't be coming over straight from work." He didn't mention the urine odor in the hallways and how all the meals smelled like boiled hot dogs.

"I do think it'll be a good opportunity for you, though," she said after musing silently for a moment. She was washing dishes and he was drying. He would have preferred to wash; he enjoyed soapy hot water up to his elbows—it helped his fingernails to stay clean. He thought black crescents under fingernails were unnecessarily repulsive. Similarly he disliked it when people allowed their elbows to become hard grey patches—like scales, he thought, the only place where man forgot to evolve from reptile—and he secretly took hand cream from his stepmother's bathroom to apply to his own arms.

"How is it an opportunity?" he asked. "There's no chance for advancement."

She finished the last pot. They'd had a spaghetti dinner. The family was Italian. The grandparents had immigrated seventy years ago.

She said, "Now you can adopt yourself some grandparents. You can choose your own new grandpa, since you no longer have a real one." She was draining the dishwater and sponging the counter.

"I don't have a phony one anymore either."

"You know what I meant."

The sink made a sucking noise.

*Grandpa DiMartino was eighty-five years old and toothless. He hadn't worn his dentures in twenty years. They didn't fit right. But no one in the family considered his naked gums a sign of age. He just cut his meat thinner and scraped his corn off the cob with a knife. He seldom sat down at the table to eat, but always seemed to be in the kitchen preparing the next course. At home spaghetti was a meal in itself, but to Grandpa pasta was common, just an appetizer, something for peasants who didn't want to feel hungry anymore. After the pasta came the meat—pork chops or rolled roast—and eggplant or zucchini, then the salad prepared with olive oil and vinegar, oregano, garlic. Still more: fruit and cheese, walnuts and almonds. Finally there were honeycakes and coffee, and Grandpa would*

63

*tell jokes while everyone sucked their sticky fingers. The blood
grandchildren often couldn't control their giggling before he
got to the punchline. Too much of that and Grandpa wouldn't
finish the story.*

*They were the same old jokes, like the same olive-oil-and-to-
mato-sauce smell in the kitchen, the drowsy comfort of watching his big color television in the living room while hearing his
triumphant "Ahhh" in the dining room as he slapped down a
winning card in bridge.*

*His eyes were bright as he looked down the Christmas table:
four children, four children-in-law, eleven grandchildren, one
blond adopted grandson, three great-grandchildren in atten-
dance. He called to the other end of the table, through steam
rising from the pasta, to his wife, Nana: "Hey, me and you —
we started all this trouble."*

*But that couldn't be entirely true, unless he wasn't counting
me.*

The ward had only fourteen men, two rooms of four each and
one dormitory space with six beds. One of the smaller rooms
housed the bedridden: they never left their mattresses, but
were outfitted with tubes and jars for bodily functions, and
were spoon-fed three times a day, and were turned on the hour
to prevent bedsores. Their beds could be cranked to an angle,
so they appeared to be sitting up, and usually the television was
on in the room, cartoons or exercise shows. Their heads would
loll back on their pillows. Usually their eyes were shut. There
were times when Mr. Feldon would shout, a long glissandoed
"Ohhhh," but if one of the men who could push his own
wheelchair was in that room — because that was the best television — he would shout back, "Shut up!" The other three beds
were silent, except near mealtimes when they occasionally
whimpered. On their more active days they would pick at their
catheters or detach the bags and spill urine all over themselves,
then sleep until they were found sticky and reeking. Their frail

old bones would have to be seated in a shower chair and tied there with a diaper restraint, one that came up between the legs and tied around the waist to the back of the chair. Then into their private shower, where they could be hosed off. Next, a nurse had to rethread the catheter. Phelan would have to hold the wrinkled elderly phallus while the nurse inserted the tube.

The other residents of the ward were free to roam the halls in the daytime. They could park their wheelchairs anywhere; or if they were walkers — dragging their feet on the carpet, using a cane and holding the handrails which lined every hall — they found plenty of vinyl love seats spaced conveniently against the wall in the lobby and also in the recreation area. And there were straight-backed chairs in the dining room where some old guys went right after breakfast (which was served in their rooms) to wait for lunch. The men's and women's wards were not really separated, other than room assignment. The men's rooms were all clumped together at the end of one hall. They shared the same lobby and rec room and dining area, and they treated each other as equals. Mr. Scovasso would bark, "Hey there, out of my way," or "Watch where you're going, stupid," to man and woman alike, and he'd prod their ribs with his cane, usually causing the victim to put up some sort of complaint, whatever they were capable of, and Phelan would have to break up the fight and send each on their way again. The old ladies often got their wheelchairs caught in the doorways, and the old men would be annoyed by the doorway being blocked. More than once, one of the girls was struck on her head with a walking stick, which most of the men carried, regardless of whether they actually walked or used a wheelchair. Then the grumbling fellow would have to be punished, taken back to his room for the afternoon, while he protested the lack of consideration shown by all these old people he had to live with.

"But you can't go around hitting anyone who inconveniences you," Phelan would reason with Mr. Scovasso.

65

"I will if they don't get outta my way."

But sometimes Mr. Scovasso seemed happy, and he would whisper in a loud voice that Willie Beeman was wandering around the private ward again, "Up with the rich dames," he would say, "and I wanna see the fireworks." Everybody knew that when Willie got tired of wearing his urine-soaked trousers, he would pull them down, underwear too if he was wearing any, and continue his aimless walk around the halls with his pants jumbled around his ankles.

Willie walked continuously—never raised his feet from the rug, but pushed them forward one at a time, inching his way along. And he never held the handrails; his hands were always clasped in front of himself—whether his pants were pulled up or not—like a little shield in front of his genitals. It was Phelan's idea to use suspenders, and on top of them to pin Willie's pants to his shirt, because it distressed some of the visitors to see him there without pants.

Phelan's shift started at four o'clock, cigarette time for the smokers. They would begin to assemble early, so when he came in from the time clock next to the kitchen—which smelled of hot dogs and mashed potatoes—there would already be an angry mob at the nurses' station. Their wheels would rub and get caught together, blocking the aisle for the others who were behind them, and someone's dress would be wound up in someone's spokes, and if either reached to try to untangle the knot, the other would slap her hand and cry, "Nurse, I can't get away." Meanwhile Mr. Scovasso would be announcing, several times, that it was after four and a man needs a good smoke in the afternoon while he reads his paper; but Mr. Scovasso wasn't allowed a newspaper while he smoked. It was too dangerous.

Some of them needed help with their cigarettes, so Phelan held their ashtray in his lap and gathered four wheelchairs around himself in the hall—three women and a man, Mr. Timm. He had to always be aware of which cigarette was whose. One at a time he held a burning cigarette to their eager mouths, let them suck in the smoke, then returned that cigarette to the ashtray and picked up the next. They would cup his hand as he held their cigarette to their lips. But he had to watch, while helping one, that the others didn't grab for the ashtray, or with their unsteady hands they might dump all the burning butts into his crotch.

Phelan had to watch Mr. Scovasso to make sure he didn't try to take his cigarette into the rec room or dining hall. He would never leave a good discussion, so Phelan came to work prepared with a topic to keep Mr. Scovasso talking during the cigarette break. It was during one of these breaks that Phelan and Mr. Scovasso together decided that unemployment could be cured by making all those lazy people and crazy students go to work solving some of the world's problems, like eliminating pollution and traffic jams by making sidewalks that worked like escalators, and making money for the government by sending scriptwriters, actors, and movie cameras out into space to make movies while they're up there doing tests.

*It was an Old World family, the head of it being the sire of sires, and although it wasn't like an Indian tribe gathering around the old chief for his wisdom, everyone had something to say to or ask from Grandpa, from how did he cook the zucchini, to why did he think men landing on the moon would bring an end to the earth — where in the Bible did it say that? He answered most of the comments (shouting almost always). The ones he didn't respond to, he might not have heard. He became angry when the brown-eyed grandchildren said someone had called them wops. "You tell them your father fought in War Number Two." Unfortunately that answer was no good when someone was called a bastard. Grandpa didn't know about that. He was never alone so I could tell him.*

There were always annoying interruptions during the cigarette conversation, like Birdie Newland who wheeled herself up and down the halls all day, calling for help, over and over, even if no nurse or aide was near. She asked the kitchen workers and the housekeepers, and she asked the other patients, "Help me, please, won't someone help me." She kept moving and toured the entire hospital several times a day, propelling her chair along by pulling on the handrails. So at any time in the middle of a conversation, she might pass by, asking for help. Her calls were never loud. Mr. Scovasso shouted back, "Shut up, you crazy old loon." Someone had put a sign on the back of her chair saying HELP WANTED.

"Ignore her," Phelan told Mr. Scovasso. But Phelan couldn't stop him from getting up — cigarette in his teeth — and going after Mrs. Newland. He pushed her chair, sending her down the hall and out of earshot. "Stay away from me," he warned her.

"Can't you just ignore her?" Phelan said when Scovasso came back to the ashtray.

"I take things into my own hands. That's leadership, boy. Don't put up with any nonsense and you won't get any. Ran my home that way; I've two fine sons with respect for the name they carry and the family law, worked in the family business till they graduated college . . . or almost." He set his jaw and raised his chin.

The routine continued: All the men needed to go to the toilet before supper. One by one, Phelan had to take them to the bathroom. The smokers could go first (because Phelan knew where they were), except Scovasso, who took himself and always demanded that he be allowed to shut the door, even though that was against regulations. Mr. Scovasso said he still stood to pee, but the others had to be helped onto the toilet, which was equipped with handrails; their penises had to be tucked between their legs, pointing downward, so they wouldn't get themselves wet. Some of them were heavy to lift out of their chairs. Phelan had to bend to put his arms under theirs and clasp his hands together between their shoulder blades, stand and lift to raise their butts off their seats while he kicked the wheelchair away. Then he had to tell them, "Hold on," and make sure their arms were around his neck while he let go to unzip and push their pants down before he sat them on the toilet.

Besides Mr. Scovasso, they were all beyond being ashamed, either chuckling or clicking their dentures and saying without bitterness, "Imagine needing help . . . at my age," or sitting silently, their bony hands on the handrails, their shoulders slightly raised as though shrugging, and their murky, bewildered eyes staring at him.

After toileting, he took them all to the dining area. He rushed them down the halls in their wheelchairs, faster than they could go on their own, pushed them up to a table and locked the wheels. At the same time he would point the walkers, like Willie Beeman, in the proper direction and tell them to go. While going back and forth from the men's wing to the dining hall with wheelchairs, he called encouragement to the walkers as he passed them. But Willie Beeman would walk past the dining room door and continue down the hall to the women's wing if Phelan wasn't right there to turn him through the doorway.

The cart from the kitchen carrying all the filled dinner trays arrived through the back door of the dining room. It was Phelan's job to make sure each of his men got the proper tray. They were all labeled, no salt or low salt, pureed or chopped, or (in a few cases) regular. Mr. Scovasso took his meal in the rec room and watched comedy reruns while eating. No cartoons; he called them foolishness for old fools. Phelan would take Scovasso's tray to him first, so the food wouldn't be cold. Scovasso was one of the few who noticed if it was, and he would complain loudly about it. He said he refused to eat with all those senile old farts, and he ardently enjoyed the comedies on the tube. A few of the women ate in there also, the ones who dressed themselves and preferred not to have anyone else spill a tray onto their laps.

Cockroaches were a problem, so there was a rule that only the bedridden ate dinner in their rooms. There would be another cart with four dinner trays waiting at the doorway of that room. A few of the men inside would be bawling for their food, sounding like the low groans of cattle. These four had pureed dinners: always an ice-cream scoop of mashed potatoes, then a puddle of something else, usually green, and a lump of something brown, the meat, all the same texture as their diarrhea.

Phelan cranked their beds up so their heads were slightly higher than their bellies—so gravity might help them swallow —and sat beside them on the mattress, feeding them spoonful by spoonful.

They always opened their withered pink mouths eagerly and ate without opening their eyes. The green and brown would liquefy in their mouths as they chewed with their tongues, and little rivers of it would run from the corners of their lips, which would have to be caught with the spoon before it reached the pillow case. The television would continue to chatter, news or talk shows.

After supper was bedtime for most of the hospital. These four were already in bed, but they had to be washed and their pajamas changed. He took off their pajamas but left the shirts under their heads, necks and shoulders, to catch any of the bathwater from dampening the sheets. Their faces and necks and especially in and behind the ears had to be washed because the day shift might not have cleaned them after lunch if some of the food had dripped down their cheeks and into their ears, where it would have dried during the afternoon and become crusty.

During this time there was a bingo game in the dining room for patients who still knew how to play and were allowed to stay up for an hour or two after supper. Someone else ran the bingo game. Phelan requisitioned some lotion for the bedridden room and applied it behind their ears and to hotspots on their elbows. When they were bathed and dressed in clean pajamas, their tubes secure, lights out, Phelan said good-night.

Mr. Scovasso would be waiting in his room with his newspaper. He undressed himself and put on his dotted pajamas. He always folded his clothes and put them on the chair beside his bed if they were clean. Someone would have to sneak his socks into the hamper because he griped about the waste of unnecessary washing, and how no one can get socks dirty puttering around carpeted halls. Still, he wouldn't wear dirty clothes, and even threw away a shirt now and then, if he'd spilled something on it. "I won't wear a dribble-cloth like these old coots," he said if a nurse found the shirt and tried to rescue it from the trash. Then he would tear it—hold it with his teeth and rip it clean in half—and they'd leave it in the trash after that.

He had a clean-shaven face and a smile with teeth, and his skin was still tinted olive. His hair, not yet pure white, he combed straight back, and sometimes it got too long, curling down behind his ears, because he wouldn't let the nurses shave his neck every month when they made the rounds with the electric clippers. He proudly wore his glasses every day, and left them on while the newspaper was read to him. He wore slippers and a bathrobe, and wouldn't get under the covers; he sat on the edge of the bed with his feet on the floor. He had a nightstand with a large whiskey-bottle lamp, a clock which he wound every night and a box of tissues in a dispenser.

Phelan sat in a chair beside Scovasso's bed in the dormitory, the paper flat on his knees, scanning the headlines on the front page.

"Nothing from there," Scovasso directed. "They always lie on that page. Scandal sheet."

"Okay." Phelan turned the page. "Well the president says–"

"No, I don't care about that. I want news, boy. Sayin' ain't happenin'. Read me some facts of action."

"Action . . . okay, bank robberies? Two armed gunmen escaped with—"

"No, I can see that on television any day. You know, boy," he leaned close, "it ain't true what's on television. They make it up."

"But it's true here."

"Can't tell, boy, can't trust 'em. Could've made it up or watched it on television themselves."

"Well, there ought to be something real in here, let's see...." He folded back the first two pages. "A fire downtown, an old apartment building, three a.m., four engines responded, evacuation of fifty-three residents."

Mr. Scovasso waved that one aside. "They been puttin' out fires as long as I can remember and before that too. That ain't news. They fill this paper with talk and everyone's scraped knees."

"Here's something, then, a gang fight in the South Bay. A hundred youths from two area Chicano gangs clashed in a used car lot."

"Kids' games," Mr. Scovasso grumbled. He cleared his throat and spit into a tissue.

"How about the stock market?"

"No — buncha crooks. I never dealt with 'em and still lost my first house." He slumped a little, still sitting up though, holding onto the edge of the bed.

"You wanna lean back against the pillows, Mr. Scovasso, or get into bed?"

"I haven't heard the news yet, let's have it."

"Okay . . . oh, says here they closed Mission Bay for up to three days — water's polluted, and — "

"Can't prove that, another story made up. Folks readin' this paper are livin' in a fool's paradise, that's all."

Phelan scanned the comics, then turned the page. "Well, an American just defeated the Russian champion at Mr. Potato-head."

"That so?"

"Yeah, a new record too — 117 different variations."

"That'll show 'em." He swung his feet. His ankles were pale and blue-veined.

Phelan pulled the covers down and took Scovasso's slippers off, and the old man swung his legs onto the bed, clutching at the sheets, but remained seated upright. Phelan sat on the bed with the newspaper.

"How about this: A two-year-old girl in Lakeside made a pair of wings out of chicken feathers collected from her backyard and flew all the way to Vegas."

He nodded stoutly. "That's the American way, always a new frontier to explore, always'll be something no one's ever seen or done before." He lay back against his pillow. "Go on."

"Well, this computer dating company is getting sued because they were programming robots to fit the descriptions of the type of date the customers were requesting. One girl married the robot before she found out. . . . Seems he was programmed for only a month, stopped functioning . . . on their wedding night."

"That's more like it." Scovasso's eyes were closed. Phelan stood and turned off the lamp and took Scovasso's glasses off. All his roommates were already sleeping, wheezing, snorting, coughing. . . .

"And the president of Mercury says immigrants will be welcome starting this summer, and it's always summer there." Phelan watched the old man sleeping. Scovasso hadn't had any visitors since Phelan had been hired, probably longer; the old man didn't say.

Before he left, Phelan pulled the drapes. The morning aide would open them again, before sunrise, and the light would be there all day. It wasn't a dim, dark hospital. There were many large windows, at least one per room, and all the doors to the outside were glass. There were some sliding glass doors too — kept locked so they became glass walls.

# 17

## LION HUNTING

From up ahead, just over the next small hill, there are additional voices. More crickets, and now other bugs that buzz continuously like electric wires, and frogs. But before he reaches the creek, he comes to the trees. Five old pines stand in a cluster with just enough room between them for a house. The house is gone, not even a cement foundation left, if it even had one. It was probably too long ago for that. The trees had been brought in — perhaps as seedlings or maybe just the seeds — and planted around the house to make this look like somewhere else. He pauses near the trees. The trunks with large, frozen, clear-yellow drips of sap, and the limbs overhead and the needles on the ground fill this area with the husky scent of pine. It always did seem like somewhere else. The rest of the hills are nearly without odor, except when the buckwheat dries or near one of the few sage bushes or after it rains.

This is where he used to bring his chessboard.

*It's no good trying to play a real game with yourself; you always know exactly what you're thinking, every advance can be thwarted, it's a perfect stalemate. What's the point; why did I ever used to do it?*

All the land is light now, and the sky slightly pale blue, but still no sun. Colors are subdued, blending into each other, still close to black-and-white. But even in daylight, competitive bright colors are not natural here. The flowers are all earth-toned, the weeds and grass are only green during the rainy season's three months.

Out on the path near the five trees, he once met a king snake. It was early summer and the snake was very young, no longer than his forearm. The snake had been moving down the path and he was coming up, and they stopped when they met. The snaked dodged Phelan's hands, coiling and standing upright with half its body, opening its mouth, but silent. Phelan was wary, managing to keep the snake at bay but unable to get his hands on it from behind so the snake couldn't bite. The snake wanted to get away, but didn't turn away from the trail and escape into the bushes, as it could've. The way Phelan caught it was to drop a handful of pine needles over the snake, then run down the path until he found a discarded paper cup, return to scoop the needles and snake into the cup and pinch the rim of the cup closed. But it was late and Phelan had to go back to the house before dark, so he let the snake go right where they'd met. Instead of immediately going into the bushes, the snake coiled and stood up again, opening its mouth. Phelan smiled and turned away. On the way home he was always facing the sunset over the landscaped western hills with the skyline of palms and fir trees black against the red and orange sky. And even the rocks and grass in the eastern hills were tinted.

# 18

## TEMPORARY WORK

*Before Grandpa DiMartino was sick, the family gatherings were centered around him. All those people shouting to be heard, Grandpa in the thick of it, half English, half Italian, half cursing. There was a knack to being heard and being able to participate, and if you didn't have it, you could only listen and watch, or go somewhere and play solitaire. Grandpa sometimes played cards with all the grandchildren at once, gathered around a big table. He always played to win, never cheating to allow one of us the victory. It might've been fun to face him in double solitaire, but he never played anything less than four-handed games.*

They were going to talk about old sci-fi space movies, and Phelan had brought a radio so they could hear the ball game, but Mr. Scovasso wasn't waiting at the nurses' station for his cigarette. There wasn't time to go searching for him because a nurse had already doled out the pack, without matches, and the smokers were holding out their cigarettes. He asked the nurse at the station preparing the evening medicines, "Where's Mr. Scovasso?"

"Probably still in the rec room. I think he's been in there all day."

Right on schedule, Mrs. Newland was coming slowly down the hall, holding the handrails and pulling herself along in her wheelchair, chanting, "Help me, oh someone help me. . . ."

"What do you need, Birdie?" the nurse called without looking up from the medicine tray.

"Just help me, won't someone help me. . . ."

"You're okay, Birdie," the nurse said.

"Oh yes, oh someone help me. . . ."

Phelan said, "Does she need to go to the toilet? I'll take her."

The nurse smiled. "She's on a catheter."

The more experienced staff called that "getting caught." During Phelan's first week, a lady had asked him to wheel her chair out the glass door in the lobby because she had to catch the bus to Denver. The receptionist had stopped Phelan on his way out with her. "No, Mrs. Hale, you're not going anywhere." Then looking at Phelan, "Yesterday she thought she could crawl out an air vent. You'll see pretty quickly, some of these patients are pretty well out of touch with reality." Bringing Mrs. Hale back to her room, he'd noticed she hadn't been taking a suitcase with her.

It just took experience to avoid "getting caught": knowing what was routine and what wasn't. Mrs. Newland's calls were joined by a man shouting in the rec room: "Help me, help me, dammit."

The nurse hummed a tune softly, raising a small plastic jigger up level with her eyes as she measured some red liquid into it.

Phelan was sweating. He finished the cigarettes and stamped the butts out with three or four puffs left in them. The smokers didn't notice. The huddle started to break up, the usual traffic jam with footrests caught in spokes or two chairs face-to-face, unable to turn.

The drapes were open in the rec room, exposing the whole sliding glass door, so almost half of the room was a large cube of sunlight crowded with swimming dust. The television was tuned in to afternoon cartoons, and one other patient was in the room — a lady with her wheelchair pulled to the bookcase. Around her chair, on the floor, were all the books from the middle shelf, and she was reaching for more, her hand moving with extreme slowness for another book from the half-empty second shelf.

Mr. Scovasso was slumped on the couch in his pajamas and bathrobe, silent. He hadn't shaved and had neglected to wear his glasses. His eyes were closed.

"Hey there," Phelan said, parking the sleeping Mr. Timm in front of the television. He turned the sound down.

Another book fluttered to the floor next to the lady's wheelchair.

"Did you watch the news today? The moon shot's set for next month, y'know."

"You go away and leave me alone." Scovasso didn't open his eyes.

Phelan watched the set for a moment: A hillbilly with a long grey beard flying over his shoulder was chasing a puppy who ran upright on two legs; the hillbilly, with a hatchet raised over his head, was yelling, "I'll getcha if it's the last thing I do," a tiny, crackly voice. They passed the same houses and trees over and over.

"You were calling for help."

"Go away."

Phelan sat on the arm of the couch, his back to Mr. Scovasso, but turned sideways a little, arms folded, and said over his shoulder, "You want a cigarette? You can smoke in here if you want today. You need a cigarette?"

"Let me watch television."

A couple of encyclopedias fell out of the bookcase together, one landing in the lady's lap. She stared at it, then pushed it to the floor also. It landed face down, crushing its onionskin pages.

A lion was conducting a symphony and the tuba player's cheeks were round and red.

"I wanted to talk about something, Mr. Scovasso."

"All talk. Always talk. People always talk."

"You like to talk."

"Shut up." Then Mr. Scovasso tipped his head over the back of the couch, face to the ceiling, his eyes still shut, his eyelids almost transparent, like wax paper. He hollered, "Help me, damn-you-all-to-hell!"

The lady held her ears. A mouse was playing the bass drum and an elephant the triangle.

Then it was quiet. Phelan asked, "What do you need?"

"Get out."

"I want to tell you something."

A few magazines splatted on the floor.

"You don't have to answer, just listen if you want to." He still had his back to Mr. Scovasso, but his head was half turned, so he could watch the television and glance at Scovasso now and then. "I thought you might like to hear about my family, like my grandfather. Man, could he ever cook."

"Don't call me *man*."

Phelan cleared his throat. "We were all afraid of him when we were little, cause his voice was so gruff, and when we would cry, he'd say, 'I'll give y'a nickel if you cry.' And we would stop."

"Fools and bastards . . ."

Phelan swallowed and blinked. "It does seem funny, doesn't it, but we never wanted that nickel. I'm not sure why — "

"Just get out — "

"Anyway," Phelan's voice struggled under Scovasso's, "I thought of you because my grandfather lost a house too, and he had to move and sell pennants and trinkets at state fairs, and — "

"Help me, one of you bastards help me!"

Some picture books went down next, colored photographs of Tahiti and the Pacific reefs. A space-age mouse with a plastic bubble over his head and ears, and moon-boots on his feet, was chased by a cat, whiskers and all in his own plastic bubble, passing the same craters over and over. "I'll get you, you little—"

Phelan turned away from the television. He looked straight ahead, out of the rec room door, into the fluorescent hallway.

"Shut up and get out." Scovasso threw a pillow, hitting Mr. Timm in the back of the head. Mr. Timm opened his eyes and began watching the space race.

Phelan lowered his eyes and watched the toe of his sneaker draw invisible circles on the floor, then he wrote some invisible words, HI THERE.

*I don't think we ever saw Grandpa in pajamas or a bathrobe, nor lying in bed, except once when he took a nap fully dressed on the couch. Also there'd been an open casket. Most everyone cried quite a bit and almost everybody was hugged at least once.*

Phelan played an invisible game of tic-tac-toe with his sneaker on the floor. He swallowed again.

After a while he stood and said, "I'll tell you later, okay? I'd better go toilet those guys in bed."

There was an advertisement for the Hideaway Inn in Las Vegas, where the sand was warm and the slots hot. Scovasso never opened his eyes. "I'm not the one who's going to the moon."

Phelan washed his face and hands, and his eyes looked out of the mirror, murky and out of focus.

By this time the medication nurse was whistling in the non-ambulatory room as she pushed a catheter up Mr. Feldon's penis. "Sheets'll need to be changed here," she said. "We leaked a little, didn't we Mr. Feldon."

"Sorry I wasn't here sooner," Phelan said. "I was checking on Mr. Scovasso."

"Yes, he's had a rough day."

"Has something happened?" Perhaps bad news from home, the murder of one of Scovasso's prized sons, some syndicate war, treachery within the family business, swindled and bankrupted by a faithful partner.

"Well . . ." her voice was breezy, "nothing important. He wet his bed last night. We've been teasing him about it just to let him know it's no big deal."

"I don't think that's going to work."

"Apparently not. Put a rubber mat under Mr. Feldon's sheets." She went into the bathroom and washed her hands. "The urinary tract sometimes gives out first. The muscles there are used as much as the heart, over a lifetime, and sometimes it's just a question of which is going to go first."

"It could've just been an accident."

"Could've." She left the room, pushing her little cart of medicines back up the hall.

Mr. Scovasso didn't touch his dinner, and by the time the kitchen aide had picked up his tray, he'd gone to his room and gone to bed. His newspaper, which had been delivered as usual, was still rolled and bound with a rubber band, and he'd kicked it off the end of the bed when he put his feet under the covers. Phelan picked it up and smoothed it flat and put it on the nightstand for Mr. Scovasso to read in the morning.

Phelan had an upstairs apartment and the top half of a tree was his view. When he couldn't sleep at night, he lay and watched the tree make pictures of faces, horses, dogs, space aliens and unnamed shapes with its branches, framed by the window. Over the weekend he went to his stepparents' house and looked at photo albums, mostly pictures from the time before they'd gotten him.

# 19

## TEMPORARY WORK

In the course of a week Mr. Scovasso's hands started shaking so badly he could hardly hold a fork. The nurses made him eat with spoons so he wouldn't poke his eyes out. Then he complained of an upset stomach and couldn't keep anything down, especially the hot dogs on Wednesday. They gave him baby food for a day and a half and sent him to bed when he became short of breath every time he stood up to change the channel on the television.

Phelan said it was just coincidence. "Wait, he doesn't need a doctor," he said to the nurse as she dialed. "He's just depressed. He'll get over it."

"And what do you think happens to old people when they get depressed," the nurse said.

*One of my uncles went to a spa where he worked out with equipment and weights. Grandpa called it baloney. The muscular uncle's wife was one of Grandpa's daughters. She laughed and said, "I never saw you do a single exercise, Pop." Everyone was in Grandpa's backyard, in lawn chairs gathered around a table with figs and cheese, bread and salami, olives and pickled peppers. The adults drank red wine and the kids had a little wine diluted in lemon-lime. Several conversations were going on. Father and his brother were talking about rabbit hunting in Mexico. Some of the aunts were talking about some of the cousins. Nana was singing to a sleeping baby in her lap. Then the conversation focused on the muscular uncle's claim that unless you worked out, you lost your muscles quickly. The uncle's wife agreed with her husband. Father said his muscles got plenty of workout digging rocks out of the garden. There weren't enough lawn chairs; some of the kids kneeled on the grass. Grandpa said he could do an exercise if he wanted to. The uncle said, go ahead, try it. Some of the aunts thought he shouldn't, so they assured Grandpa that he was in great shape. But Grandpa waved aside all the comments and got down on the ground. The uncle gave a few instructions, and soon Grandpa was doing pushups. "Count, count, how many have I!" he called, but everyone was shouting and laughing; someone yelled "One hundred!" when Grandpa was up to eight. Grandpa went back to his chair and the conversation broke into pieces again. Grandpa started arguing with an aunt about the proper way to roast a bell pepper.*

The doctor came. He had already arrived when Phelan got to work on Friday. Phelan went straight to Scovasso's room. The nurse was there too. Scovasso had his eyes shut, several blankets up to his chin. His mouth made a slightly puckered scowl, but otherwise his face was plain and pale, saying nothing.

The doctor was not young, but not too old. He didn't flirt with nurses. "A completely bland diet from now on," the doctor said. "Little sugar and no more salt, go easy on the starches, no more heavy fiber."

The nurse wrote it down.

"And keep him warm, no more short sleeves. Also no more walking."

Phelan stepped closer. "Until when?" The old man never moved; even his breathing couldn't be detected through the pile of blankets. The doctor looked at Phelan. "From now on."

The nurse dabbed sweat on Scovasso's brow. "The fever's probably breaking." When she finished she said, "And what about a catheter — should I put him on one?"

"Not yet." The doctor looked at his watch. "But if he has many more accidents, go ahead."

Scovasso's newspaper had been delivered, but someone had put it in the trash can next to the bed. It was still rolled with the rubber band around it. When the nurse and doctor left, Phelan took the newspaper out of the trash, but Scovasso's chocolate pudding from lunch had been dumped in the can and was all over the end of the paper.

A week later, in the rec room — late afternoon, when the after-lunch drowsiness of the hospital was just about over, an old "Superman" rerun on the set — Mr. Scovasso, one foot bare, was staring at the slipper which had fallen off, just beyond his reach.

Scovasso was on the couch. Phelan saw an empty wheelchair with Scovasso's name written on the back, crooked, with an ink marker.

"Why do you just stand there?" Mr. Scovasso said. "Help me."

Phelan picked up the slipper.

"Well, put it on me. How'm I gonna get anywhere."

"Does this mean you're feeling better? Good, because I have an idea."

The old man was wearing his glasses again, but they were smeared with greasy fingerprints, his eyes blurred and magnified. Then he said, "I gotta go before they find out and come here."

"*They,* Mr. Scovasso?"

Scovasso stared. "Who are you?"

Phelan looked down at the slipper in his hand.

"Gimme the shoe, boy, I gotta go."

Phelan put the slipper down on Scovasso's legs. Scovasso glanced down at it for a moment, then turned his attention to the television, where a few freckled kids were kneeling on a sidewalk with battery-powered moon-mobiles, batteries not included.

After a few minutes Mr. Scovasso abruptly batted the slipper off his lap with a backhanded slap. It skidded under the television.

"I would never let my kids watch the tube," Scovasso said. "We had a business to run. Day and night."

The two of them sat and watched the screen. Afternoon cartoons started. "These new cartoons are so bad," Phelan said. "The animation is so phony." He turned to Scovasso who was staring into his own lap, watching a wet spot grow.

"Hey! wait, stop!"

Scovasso sighed and looked back at the screen. The same cat-and-mouse chase, this time on board a ship, passing smokestack after smokestack.

"Come on," Phelan said, "we've gotta change your pants. We can't let the nurses see this. Come on, let's use your chair, it's faster." He took Scovasso's hand and pulled him off the couch, turned him around, then pushed the wheelchair up behind him.

"When will the music start? Is this my seat?" Scovasso asked.

"Yes!" Phelan looked around the room, then hurried to the bookcase and took some encyclopedias, the S, M and R volumes, brought them over and stacked them in Scovasso's lap. "Don't worry, no one'll see the spot."

They passed the smokers at the nurses' station, then went into Scovasso's room. Phelan took the books and put them on Scovasso's nightstand.

"Take off your pants." He pulled the curtain around Scovasso's bed and took a clean pair of trousers out of a drawer.

"Come on, Mr. Scovasso, take off your pants so you can put the clean ones on. No one'll know, don't worry."

"Help me."

"You can do it yourself."

Scovasso fumbled with his zipper. His hands shook. "No, no, they'll find out!"

"No they won't Mr. Scovasso, I promise." Phelan tugged Scovasso's pants off from the ankles, then had Mr. Scovasso stand to step into the clean ones. "Do it yourself. Here, hold them." Scovasso finally sat down, panting, and Phelan zipped the zipper. "Next time ask for help before you need to go. I'll take you to the bathroom. You can close the door."

Scovasso said, "I'll be leaving anyway, tonight or tomorrow. They're not gonna find me and throw rocks again."

"Where are you going?"

"Doncha know, boy?"

"Don't worry, I'll get you to the bathroom in time." He sat down and picked up one of the encyclopedias. There was a silence and he could hear Scovasso breathing. Phelan cleared his throat, traced the title of the book with his index finger, looked up, looked back down, glanced out the window. Scovasso was still breathing, the same sound, the same rhythm. The clock ticked. Phelan took a breath and said, "Don't you wish you could go to the moon?"

"Who's going there?"

"The American astronauts, remember?" Phelan showed Scovasso a picture of a space suit in the book. "They have to do a lot of training before they go up there." Another picture showed an astronaut inside a capsule, surrounded by controls and little lights.

"I'll be going to my hideout . . . any day now. The lights in my eyes won't hurt this time, candles and music before he ever said he was sorry. Not this time."

Phelan stared at a page with two pictures, a rocket blasting off and a capsule bobbing in the ocean.

"It's time for a smoke," Scovasso said.

"I was thinking you should quit smoking, it's not good for you."

"He didn't say I couldn't have my cigarettes."

The next picture was the control room where men sit behind panels of lights with television screens and talk to the astronauts. Mr. Scovasso looked out the window.

*Before the Great Depression, Grandpa DiMartino was a jewelry importer in Brooklyn, specializing in cameos of all sizes. They tried to give each of the grandchildren an antique cameo after the funeral. There were almost enough to go around. Nana wore a necklace Grandpa had given her before they were married. Grandpa said he hadn't wanted to get married. Nana laughed. "That was before," Grandpa said. This was after dinner, during coffee and liqueur, after the real cousins had left the table. "My friends asked me why I didn't go ahead and marry her," Grandpa said. He was in the kitchen putting the food away; he sent Nana back to the table to sit down. "I told them, why pay for the cow when the milk's free." Almost everyone laughed. I was too young to get it.*

When Phelan got to work he found a volunteer women's club was sponsoring activities in the rec room. He stood in the doorway staring: Several ladies were making blue tissue-paper carnations. Someone had put Mr. Scovasso next to the record player and locked his wheels. They were playing records with stories and songs. A woman was showing Mr. Scovasso the record jacket: colored cartoon figures. Mr. Scovasso's voice was gruff, but he held the album and looked at it, saying "You think I don't know about this . . ." Phelan went in and snatched the record cover away from Scovasso, hissing in his ear, "Where's your dignity?"

The whole way down the hall to his room, Mr. Scovasso sang under his breath, also while he stepped out of his wet trousers and into dry ones, "I sail and I sail on a big ocean ship with a toot . . . toot . . . out of my way."

Phelan folded his arms and tapped his sneaker silently on the floor. "I wish you wouldn't do this anymore."

And Scovasso said, "I told them when they were kids, if you can't stand the heat, get outta the fire. I'll be in my hideout in Vegas tomorrow. That goat won't follow me to the butcher shop again."

"Mr. Scovasso —"

"Lemme go, they'll find out you're holding me here!"

"Mr. Scovasso, I'm trying to talk to you. . . ." Phelan made fists. "Listen to me for a second. . . . Did anyone ever call your children names?"

Mr. Scovasso stopped singing and sat down in his chair. Phelan sat on the bed facing him. Then Scovasso handed his glasses to Phelan, and Phelan wiped the lenses with a tissue from the nightstand. Someone had stolen the clock from there.

His voice was like that of the storyteller from the record he'd heard: "I raised two fine sons and a beautiful daughter. I have seven grandchildren and four great-grandchildren. Up in Frisco. Me and my boys fished from the pier and dug clams under the bridge, and crabs . . . lots of them. We lured them into traps with fish heads. The boys learned fast and sneaked off after school to go crabbing and fish in the surf. I'd have to wallop them when they got home after dark, their mother worried sick, but we'd all eat crab the next day, or have clams with spaghetti. And the boys got better'n me — caught more fish, dug more clams. . . ." Phelan handed him the glasses and he put them on. "Can't do any of that in Frisco anymore, can't fish from the pier, no more clams under the bridge. . . . The boys are still up there. College boys, they were. One a professor now, the other draws cities. . . ."

"And the family business? . . ."

The old man lifted his hands and let them fall back into his lap. "That's gone. A fish store on Market Street."

They were silent. Then Mr. Scovasso was holding Phelan's arm. "Boy, you can help me."

"Sure, Mr. Scovasso."

"By the time they get here, I wanna be in Vegas. You can cover for me." Scovasso panted. "We got married and had babies — music and lights and everyone danced on the roofs, in the streets — everything cut up and ruined. They threw the shrimp in the gutter, so I had to kill the goat, there was no other way. He hit me. He never came back. Then she was gone. It rolled behind the stove and caught on fire. It won't happen again."

Phelan tapped his foot, then pulled the curtain around the bed and made Mr. Scovasso lie down on his back. "You'll feel better if you exercise." He lifted and lowered each of Scovasso's legs, one at a time. "I'll do it with you today, and tomorrow you can do it alone. But don't tell anyone." Then he talked to Scovasso because, he said, it's easier if you think about something else, while exercising, to drown out the pain of stiff muscles and ligaments. A nurse out in the hall remarked that Phelan was better than the story they were playing on the record player in the rec room, and Scovasso called to her, "Help!" She laughed, but Phelan went on telling Scovasso what it was like to bounce about on the moon, where there's so little gravity and nothing feels heavy. "You know what those space suits are for, Mr. Scovasso? Otherwise, your heart's so light it forgets to beat." He explained that a moon crater is a perfect place for a swimming pool, if you could keep the water from floating out and flying away.

# 20

## WORKING AT HOME

You weren't discouraged, Phelan. You picked me up — easily — and we sat on stools again. This time face-to-face. I could hardly look at you. You held my chin, kissed me quickly and said, "Did I ever mention that I know the secret of flight?"

No answer from me. You told it anyway. You were at a launching pad. A rocket was taking off. The smoke, you said, was blue and gold with green sparkles and flashes of yellow.

I felt half my size. Enough room in my clothes for a wind to blow through. A cold wind. A dry one. Well, hearing is an automatic function. Like digestion. So I heard you. Is that the same as listening? I can now repeat the tale.

So you were there when a rocket took off and the steam was a rainbow. And the thrust blew you backward. Blew you away. Out over the ocean. I think.

I didn't have to ask how you came down in one piece. You could anticipate my lame inquiries. You said you always knew that people falling through air should be able to maneuver their landing. People falling from buildings or cliffs should be able to sail a little ways at least, you said, until they found a suitable place to land. So that's what you did: maneuvered your body so you were upright in the air. Still moving forward.

See, I can recite all of this. Still moving forward because of the thrust which had sent you flying, you ran in the air. And you approached the ground. So running, you landed, and ran a ways to absorb the extra force of the fall. And there you were. You had flown. You had landed. I guess the ocean was in a different story. You landed on dry earth. And I was there, waiting, you said.

And the story was over. Somewhere in the middle of it you had handed me the paintbrush. I can't remember receiving it. You opened my fingers and slipped it in and my hand probably closed automatically. Like hearing is automatic.

I'm sweating everywhere — *everywhere* — even down here, and it itches, something else that's automatic, like scratching.

The next thing I did: I threw that brush down on the floor. A splotch of paint down there, light blue that you'd dipped the bristles into. I didn't drop the brush. I flung it down. The one thing I did do that wasn't automatic. Or was it.

# 21

## TEMPORARY WORK

Every day Phelan searched the newspaper for an article about preparations for the Apollo moon shot. He read them to Scovasso and tacked them to his bulletin board. At night he went to his stepparents' house and looked through his old books, especially his complete set of the *How and Why Wonder Books*. Just before he left, he slipped the space book and the moon book under his shirt. His stepmother would ask why he was taking them. She was saving his books for her grandchildren, so she wouldn't like him tearing out the pages with colored pictures of rockets and galaxies to pin on Scovasso's bulletin board. "You need a hobby, Mr. Scovasso," Phelan said. He'd made a plastic model of a rocket long before anyone knew what rockets would really look like. Phelan took that from his stepparents' house too and put it on Mr. Scovasso's nightstand. "My stepfather was going to help me wire this with little lights so I could have it on all night, for a night-light, and I could wake up and see this rocket flying through space. We never got around to putting the lights on, but here it is anyway." Scovasso looked out his window. It was a warm summer. Right next to the hospital was a family motel with a greenish swimming pool full of leaves and screaming kids.

"Space is what the twentieth century is all about," Phelan said. He bought a poster of the solar system and tacked it to the wall opposite Scovasso's bed.

Scovasso looked once at the model rocket. "Where are all the lights? And the music. That's where I'll be. They'll never find me this time. I'll kill a thousand goats. I'll live in Vegas."

Phelan moved between Scovasso and the window. "Get serious, Mr. Scovasso. We're trying to have a conversation."

He wouldn't chew his food properly and gagged on large pieces, so the nurses put him on a pureed diet, which he wouldn't eat, so someone had to spoon-feed him. He would bat at the spoon or block his mouth with one hand, so they started tying his wrists to the arms of his wheelchair while he ate. Then he clamped his mouth shut. The girl who was feeding him got mad and started using the spoon as a lever to force his jaw open. The food went everywhere but inside his mouth. Phelan found him in the afternoon, still tied to his chair, dried food on his face and neck, snoring with his chin down on his chest. After Phelan complained to the head nurse, the girl employee was warned. Phelan began coming to work at lunchtime to feed Scovasso, and spent the extra four hours, until his shift actually started, with him. "They're feeding me that goat, they never forgave me," Scovasso said.

Phelan didn't spoon-feed Scovasso, so he never ate, until Phelan started bringing sandwiches in his pockets. "But you can't have lunch unless you exercise afterward," Phelan said. "You don't want to be in a wheelchair the rest of your life, do you?"

Scovasso chewed with his mouth open. "I'll put my best suit in my bag and wear my old clothes, they'll never know me, they'll want to know my secret, they came in and threw all the fish into the street while they played trumpets and drums."

Phelan said, "Come on, Mr. Scovasso, this is important." Once Phelan brought a deck of cards to work. He pushed Mr. Scovasso up to a table in the rec room. "This is a game my grandfather taught us." Scovasso wouldn't pick up the hand Phelan dealt him. He looked out the glass door. Phelan could hear him breathing. After that, Scovasso lost his glasses, or somebody stole them. He stayed in bed with a fever for another week, then sat up in his chair, bundled in blankets, looking out the window. Phelan massaged his legs. "We lost a little time, last week." Scovasso coughed. He had lost ten pounds. Phelan said, "Remember, this is a secret, I want to surprise the nurses, I want you ready to walk by next week. They'll be on the moon then, you know."

Scovasso grunted. He smelled sour. "I'll need a new hat and a raincoat, it rains indoors, like the tropics, no one sleeps, I'll have a trumpet and raise a tribe and follow the salmon to Alaska."

Phelan helped Scovasso out of his chair and onto the bed. "Here we go." Phelan knelt at the foot of the bed, facing Scovasso, holding each of his ankles. He raised one leg then lowered it, raised the other then lowered it. "By yourself now." Scovasso coughed and sprayed. "Come on, Mr. Scovasso." Phelan raised one leg and lowered it, raised the other and lowered it. "You try, concentrate. You'll feel good as new."

There was a squeaking sound when Scovasso breathed. He coughed and spit. He sounded like chewing sand. His voice rasped, "They'll all want to know where I am, but they won't find me this time, they hit me with a goat, broke their mother's heart, they look for monkeys in cages at the zoo, grass is a weed but they grow it in lawns." His cough was wet and sounded like slapping.

"Calm down, Mr. Scovasso, take it easy." Phelan rubbed his chest, then lifted a leg and lowered it, lifted the other leg and lowered it.

"Help," Mr. Scovasso said.

"Shhh, I'm right here, we don't want anyone else barging in on us." Scovasso held his throat while he coughed, twelve times, his tongue curled. He spit phlegm into his pillow. "Try it yourself this time," Phelan said, "I know you can do it."

The old man's eyes watered, he coughed some more. "I asked them, how many goats hatch from a thousand eggs, they wouldn't listen." He put his hands to his face as his nose began to bleed.

Phelan looked around. He didn't have a handkerchief. "Hold on, Mr. Scovasso!" He pulled one of Scovasso's socks off and held it over his nose. "Keep your chin up." Mr. Scovasso was trying to get off the bed. "Lie still, what did you do to yourself?" Phelan dove forward, holding Scovasso down, blotting at the blood as it ran into Scovasso's mouth.

"I had to spank him," Scovasso said. "I told him but he said no and I never knew why, he hit me with a trumpet and wanted to keep it a secret, but she knew, broke her heart, I told you not to bring that goat behind the counter, they threw all the fish into the street. The goat would follow me anywhere, you came back and played your trumpet behind a cloud, she was dressed so fine, lying there, that's the last time it's going to happen, they keep fish in their living rooms in wine glasses."

Phelan, kneeling on the old man's legs, pressed the sock under his nose. "Shut up! . . . Be quiet, hold still."

"It's a nice day," Scovasso said, still coughing a little. "It was always a nice day." He spit some blood. "It was always sunny and it rained and I fed cats in the alley but wouldn't bring one home, the clouds blew across and the water sparkled, so I'm going to Vegas for a weekend in the sand, the lights never go out, I know enough to know it. I gotta pee."

The sock was caked and sticky. "Okay, good, I'll help you, just a sec." Phelan took Scovasso's other sock off and pressed it to the old man's face. Scovasso had already unzipped his pants and pulled his penis out. He began to pee, straight up, splashing across the front of Phelan's shirt, falling like a fountain back onto Scovasso. "No, stop it, stop it." Phelan grabbed the front of Scovasso's pants.

"I remember when you used to play the trumpet behind my stove," Scovasso said. "It sounded like jewels."

95

*Before anyone else in the family had a color television, Grandpa had one. All my aunts and uncles had chipped in to buy it for him. There weren't enough seats for everyone in the living room, so the kids would lie on the floor to watch. Sometimes a little one could crowd in beside Nana in her chair while she also held one on her lap. Grandpa never held any children. He never stayed in front of the set for more than five minutes. He would rather be doing something. He fixed dessert or made coffee or had to check something in the oven or carefully wrapped the garbage. But whenever someone wanted to change the channel, they had to ask him to come do it. Not that he cared what show was on, he was just afraid the knob would break off.*

The moon landing on television was after eight, so Phelan stayed at work late and took Mr. Scovasso, in his robe and slippers, into the rec room to watch it. He stood behind Scovasso with his hands on Scovasso's shoulders, and bent to tell him in his ear what they were doing and talking about on the screen. Scovasso said, "That ain't my problem, boy. Help me! There was a fire in the sink, they put squid in the drawers, I had to kill the goat."

The nurses and aides who were also gathered there to watch complained that Scovasso was talking too loud and they couldn't understand the astronauts' voices.

"Oh no, help! Somebody help! Fourteen stories and no doors or windows. I put in a new window and they threw rocks. I saw them out there, in the sunshine, hiding in a waterfall. They laughed. Nothing melted. She was never the same. Then you killed her. Don't raise your hand over me again, boy."

Then a nurse said, "Someone's peeing," so Phelan had to take Scovasso out. He brought him down to the good television in the nonambulatory room. The men there were already asleep and didn't wake when the set was turned on. Mr.

Scovasso was quiet for a while, watching a cockroach wander around on the floor beneath the set. Phelan stopped explaining what was going on. But after a while he said, quietly, "Imagine, walking in a world where nobody else has ever been." During the one-giant-leap part, he turned the sound up. The nurses up the hall in the rec room were cheering. Then Mr. Scovasso's voice came from the bathroom: "Is this the way outta here?" Before Phelan could get there, Scovasso had already tripped on the wet washcloths left on the floor. He found him on his knees, holding onto the sink.

He said, "Help."

He wasn't hurt, but after that the nurses began to keep him in his wheelchair with a vest-type restraint, tied in back and pinned so he couldn't ask another patient to loosen the knot. He began hitting people with his cane if they approached from the front, until they took that away and hid it.

# 22

## LION HUNTING

He listens for the creek. Not a sound of rushing water, just a riffle at the edges where the current folds away from the muddy banks, where the water has undermined the earth so a small ledge hangs over the creek with grass that dips blades into the surface. But he won't hear anything. The creek was dry most of the year, running only in the winter and early spring. He never knew what happened to the fish when the creek was just stones. One or two muddy pools might last until the next rainfall, but there were never any fish until spring when the county stocked the creek with minnows that ate mosquito larva.

The path crosses the creek several times. There are no bridges because the creek can be stepped over. There was a time when he hadn't been able to step across without getting his shoes wet. Now he takes off his shoes and socks but doesn't cross. He leaves his shoes on the trail and steps into the dry creek bed, following it a few yards to the first stagnant muddy pool. It's silent. The frogs hide and watch. He sits on a rock, bends over and looks into the water, but doesn't see anything, not even a reflection because it's too dark. The odor doesn't bother him. A mosquito sings in his ear and he waves it away.

*Sitting and observing a natural habitat never did work, everything just hid and waited for me to leave.*

He used to talk to them while he tried to catch them. Every day while the creek was full he was here with nets and jars. Besides the minnows and small green frogs, there were crawdads and some salamanders, bugs that skated on the surface of the water, polliwogs and dragonfly larva, and clawed frogs—large, flat, slimy frogs who never came onto land because they were clumsy and sluggish there, but in the water they could swim like eels. They had claws on each toe, which was where they got their name, since ordinary frogs have no claws.

Clawed frogs weren't native to the area nor even the continent. They came from Africa. Pet stores sold them, an exotic addition to outdoor goldfish ponds or indoor aquariums. But they would grow and eat fish, so they were flushed down toilets and found their way here. They lived under the bank of the creek where the water was darker and there was soft mud in which to bury themselves. Phelan tried to talk them out of their hiding places while he probed under the bank with a stick, waiting to see the sudden jet of cloudy water, which meant he'd flushed a clawed frog out of the mud.

He caught one once and brought it to his room to live in a jar, but it wouldn't eat. For a few days he pried the frog's mouth open with a cotton swab and pushed earthworms down its throat. Then it escaped one night and he found it in the morning on the floor, unable to move, its body dry and coated with fuzz from the rug. After he put it back into the creek, he mended an aquarium that he found in the basement and built a habitat for green frogs, minnows and crawdads. There was land and water with grass planted in the mud, and rocks making caves for the crawdads to back into, all visible from the glass sides of the aquarium. Then it turned stagnant so he dumped it out.

*But I never felt that I'd failed—I wonder why.*

In the bush nearest him, one growing next to the creek bank, there's a snarl of fishing line. He yanks it out of the bush, stripping the branches of leaves, which drop into the pool of water. He locates the end of the line and there's a silver hook, much too large to catch anything from this stream, even when it's full of water.

# 23

## TEMPORARY WORK

Whenever someone forgot to watch Scovasso for a few minutes, he would slip away, but he could always be found by one of the glass doors — the employee entrance, the lobby, the rec room or at the ends of the wings — trying to open it wide enough to get his chair through. Once they found him halfway through, his wheels caught on the doorjamb and the door itself pinning his chair like a trap. Phelan visited on weekends. He would walk all the way around the hospital, on the outside, going past each glass door until he found the one where Scovasso was sitting behind the glass. Scovasso always rapped on the glass with his knuckles and Phelan opened the door, then wheeled him around to the front and they went in the lobby. Scovasso cursed, and Phelan said it was good for him to let his aggressions out and not keep them bottled up inside waiting to explode. Then Phelan found Scovasso in his room, his wheels tied to the bedframe with a pair of socks (because the locks built onto the wheelchair were too easy to release). He had taken another patient's cane and broken the glass door which led from the rec room to the patio garden and shuffleboard courts, which nobody used. It was just a long crack, from top to bottom. "If the window wasn't so dirty, I'da gone right through it."

"You would cut yourself."

"Like air. Like smoke. Poof. There's nowhere I can't go if I want to go. Who're they to say no, I need a cigarette. The bastards are hiding in my closet, help. Find the goat before they come through the window again."

"You want to rest for a while, Mr. Scovasso?"

"Hell no."

"Sure you do." Phelan helped Mr. Scovasso into bed and raised the rails so he wouldn't fall off. Mr. Scovasso yelled for an hour while Phelan was making rounds. He was snoring and wheezing when Phelan came back.

The nurse told Phelan to keep the curtain shut in the rec room. "If he doesn't see the window, he won't know it's a way out."

Scovasso spent several hours one day sitting in a room on the private wing, refusing to leave when the old woman who lived there returned from lunch, holding onto the bathroom door-knob and bellowing as an aide tried to pull his wheelchair backward out of the room.

"What were you doing?" Phelan asked.

"Waiting for her to let me leave through there."

"The window? It doesn't open."

"A brick'll open it."

"Mr. Scovasso, you'd better stop this, they're talking about contacting your family and getting you transferred to a bigger hospital in San Francisco."

"There were rocks in my head, I spit them out, who needs stars when there're lights of every color, those bastards, those shits, those fuckers, those sons-of-bitches, you played your horn like the sun coming from behind a cloud, beautiful, beautiful. But she couldn't hear it."

Then Phelan caught him pounding on the bathroom mirror with both hands, one a flat palm, the other holding a slipper.

There weren't many objects left that he could use for tools. After the clock, the rocket on the nightstand had disappeared too. And the nurses had taken his toothbrush away.

But in another few days Scovasso managed to smash the television screen with someone else's shoe during afternoon cartoons. It started a small fire, and he cut his knee trying to put his leg through the hole in the glass. He laughed all the way to his room. And the whole time the nurse was bandaging him, he chuckled. But it wasn't the sort of laugh as though a joke had been told, nor as though he'd been tickled, nor as though he'd read a funny book or seen a funny movie. He stopped abruptly and stared out his own window until the nurse closed the curtain.

"Mr. Scovasso." Phelan sat next to him. Scovasso spit on the floor. "You've got to cut this out, I mean, windows are one thing. . . ."

"Some chickens came onto my property," Scovasso said. "I killed them and made soup."

"My stepfather used to raise chickens."

"Didja feel for the egg?" Scovasso held up his middle finger.

The day the astronauts splashed down, Phelan came in with a big photo from the newspaper of the capsule and parachute inches away from the choppy blue ocean. Someone had taken away the bulletin board — pins and tacks were too risky they said — so Phelan was taping pictures to the wall. The summer heat often made them fall and get trampled and soiled under wheelchairs.

An elderly man, but not a patient, wearing a complete suit and matching socks, was in Scovasso's room with him, cutting bread from a loaf on a TV tray. He had silvery grey hair. "I got this cheese okayed with the nurses, Pop, I think you'll like it." He put the cheese on some bread and handed it to Mr. Scovasso who took it greedily in two hands. "They said wine is okay too, Pop, just for today — for a little celebration."

"I drank wine since I was nine," Scovasso said with his mouth full. He looked out the window.

"Here, Pop." The elderly man spread a napkin in Mr. Scovasso's lap. "I brought you some new pants too. The nurse is out putting your name on them."

Phelan stood in the doorway.

The man started talking about Nicholas, Maria's youngest, who had started school last year and had tested the teacher's brain from the beginning—smart, that kid. Of course, his brother had taught him to read when he was three, so he was bored in school—of course he raised hell. Maria had him taking piano lessons and learning golf after school—just to use up some of that energy so he would go to sleep at a decent hour at night. Can you imagine, six years old and out doing nine holes after school. They'd bought a piano too. Anthony—he's pitching in Little League, the star athlete. The elderly man's son, Ralph, Maria's brother—he wasn't married yet but was handling a real fine bookstore business with his B.A. in management and a minor in English literature.

Mr. Scovasso swallowed and drank wine from a plastic punch cup. He burped and wiped his mouth, and took some more of the bread and cheese, then tried to clean a smudge off the window with his napkin. He chewed noisily, picked his teeth and leaned forward. "You know," he said, chewing as he spoke, then he had to swallow. "You should see the sons I got—two of the finest Sicilian boys ever sired. A professor, yessir, and one who decides where cities go. Yessir, fine boys, out on their own now, wish you could meet 'em."

He took another drink of wine and choked a little, so the elderly man stood up to pat his back. The man saw Phelan in the doorway. Their eyes met—Phelan's and Mr. Scovasso's son's—over the back of the old man who was bent over, coughing into his napkin. The elderly man, patting Scovasso's back, still looking at Phelan, twirled his index finger in a circle around his own ear. Phelan carefully folded the picture of the splashdown and put it into his shirt pocket.

"Come here, son," the man said. Phelan went into the room, wheeled Scovasso away from the TV tray, lifted him from his chair and laid him on the bed. Scovasso had become the easiest patient to lift. He didn't eat often, and the nurses had started giving him high-protein baby formula as a bedtime medicine.

Phelan closed the curtains.

The man said, "Is there anything he particularly needs? I don't know if there's any point to my ever coming here again, but I can leave some money to get him whatever he needs."

"He's your father," Phelan said.

The elderly man glanced at Scovasso, on his back on the bed. He had folded his hands across his chest and closed his eyes. His breathing was shallow and very quiet.

"I appreciate what you do for him here," the man said, "but that's not my father."

Phelan also looked at Scovasso — looked at him a long time before he could tell that he was still breathing.

"That man there may be the only Dominic Scovasso you've ever known, but my father was a big stern man who sat at the head of the table and tolerated no nonsense, who might hit me just for slurping my soup."

Someone out in the hall called, "Nurse . . . nurse . . . !"

"This is just some crazy old man — "

"Shut up, shut up!"

"Someday you'll understand, son."

Phelan picked up the wine bottle and held it over his head. "Get out of here."

The elderly man paused in the doorway on his way out. "I won't report you to the nurses, son, because I hope someday you see your own father — "

Phelan threw the bottle.

*We cleaned out the garage when Grandpa was in the hospital. "If we don't tell him, he'll never know the difference," one of my aunts said. Grandpa was a packrat. There were pennants from the Texas Centennial, a pogo stick, roller skates, pots and pans, countless old tools and parts of tools, boxes of trading stamps and Christmas seals, golf clubs (no one in the family golfed), a five-foot-tall plastic Santa Claus that lit up which Grandpa used to put on his porch at Christmas, a box of antique fountain pens, plates and pieces of plates that had broken long ago, pieces of jewelry, boxes of receipts, a refrigerator, a coin-operated washing machine (10 cents a load) and a regular washing machine, a washboard, a hi-fi with huge knobs, boxes of magazines no one in the family had subscribed to and paperback books no one had read. Everyone took what they wanted. They almost threw away his gas rationing stamps from World War II, calendars from 1938, 1945 and 1956 with his appointments and personal reminders, and his immigration documents. No one else wanted them.*

The door closed. Against regulations for a patient to be in his room with the door shut, but Phelan was in there, mopping up wine, sweeping up bits of glass, drying the floor then testing it with his palm for more splinters of glass. He passed his hand flat over the tiles back and forth, half the room, to be sure there was no broken glass anywhere. There was a sound, like writing on a chalkboard, and the bed was empty. Scovasso was behind the curtains trying to chop through the window with the bread knife.

"No!" Without stopping to reopen the drapes, Phelan went underneath them and grabbed Scovasso around the waist.

"They ripped all the new furniture and I'm going to cut their ears off. They'll never do it to me again."

Phelan yanked Scovasso away from the window, but tripped on the bottom of the curtains, and the two of them fell backward, pulling the curtain rod from the wall. The curtains covered them. Phelan kept one arm around Scovasso's waist as though saving a drowning man. With the other hand he tried to find an edge of the curtains. The material was full of dust and Scovasso was coughing. The knife had dropped somewhere in the folds of the curtain. Scovasso was clawing at

Phelan's fingers, trying to free himself from the lifesaver's grip. Phelan couldn't see any of Mr. Scovasso. He could hear him and feel his heartbeat against his arm. Scovasso said, "Children are born with every egg they'll ever lay, someone played the accordion and everyone danced under the bed. You wouldn't listen, I laid down the law, you raised your voice to her too, you whelp, I should've pinched your head off like a kitten."

"He's gone, it's me," Phelan gasped.

"Shut up."

Someone was paged to the phone. A nurse laughed in the hall. Phelan squirmed onto his side, kept one leg across Scovasso's body, still trapped in the folds of the curtains. The curtain rod was leaning against Phelan's neck. "Calm down, Mr. Scovasso, lie still. Everything's okay. We're in the hospital, remember?"

"That damned goat followed me, you were hungry, I turned it inside out, good as new, everyone was yelling, glass everywhere, you left with your goat and she cried for a year until they lit the candles."

"Shhh, calm down, we'll go watch TV in the rec room."

"Leave me alone. The boob tube. A waste of time."

"We've got lots of time—"

"No—the grass is neck-high in the bathroom, the kids are old men, the candles had to be blown out or they'd start the tree on fire, but there's plenty of lights, all they wanted was to dance in the freezer, that's where I kept the squid." He bit Phelan's arm through the curtain. His legs were treading water. "Don't let it start again. I promised I'd be on the glass elevator tonight before the doors shut, where I can hear all the lights. It's lost down the drain. There were so many candles and a thousand trumpets, you came too late, the store is lost, the blood was everywhere, the goat followed me there, you were hungry, she said no, the chickens were gone, I couldn't catch a cat, she kept goldfish in the sink, she could've forgiven if you'd come home before they lit the candles and played the trumpets in the balcony."

"Mr. Scovasso, think, concentrate. You've still got me."

"No! You hit me, you raised your hand against your father and killed your mother."

"I didn't. I didn't! But I will if you don't shut up!"

Scovasso screamed like a woman. His fingernails dug into Phelan's arm. His body worked as though convulsing. But then his voice became steady. "Please, boy, let me go."

Phelan lay still for a moment, then uncovered his head, pushed the curtains aside and got off the floor.

Scovasso was sitting in his wheelchair, looking out the window. He was cleaning a pair of glasses, but there was no glass in the frames, just his thumb and finger rubbing together where the glass should be.

It wasn't much later, still before dinner, when Scovasso used the knife he'd hidden under his bed to cut his restraints. He walked out the lobby door. No one was watching for an attempted escape by a man upright on two legs.

Phelan claimed he wasn't in Scovasso's room at the time.

"Imagine him," a nurse said, "hungry and no way to eat, lost and confused, he may walk out into traffic or be picked up as a drunken bum. And when it gets dark, he'll be cold and scared."

Phelan smiled.

The nurse grew taller and thinner. Her hand shook, pointing down the hall, vaguely toward the kitchen or the time clock. "You finish your shift then don't bother coming back. We don't need unsympathetic people caring for our patients, we don't need you around here!"

The whole hospital had pricked up their ears. Even the patients seemed to stay awake longer in front of the new television in the rec room, and they looked at each other, patients who'd never before acknowledged all the others like themselves who lived there together. The radios were all turned on every half-hour for the local news broadcasts, but no station ever included Scovasso in its headlines. Phelan stripped Scovasso's bed and took all the space posters off the walls. Dinner was silent, and no one spilled nor peed on the floor. The patients went to bed and lay awake, staring at the ceiling. Phelan sat on Scovasso's bed and stared at his nightstand where the clock and lamp and model rocket and box of tissues had been. It was bare now, except for a plastic tray and a rectal thermometer. He was sure he could hear Scovasso's clock somewhere.

The night was full of stars. There were no curtains to close.

In his own bed, alone that night, Phelan tried to bury his ears in the pillows, but the noise of the helicopter hovered around him, fading then returning then fading again, and he might've slept a little, but dreamed he was awake and trying to sleep. He tossed and twisted his sheets and sweated and kicked the sheets away. And when the helicopter returned, he opened his eyes, realizing he wasn't being awakened. He stared at his ceiling, a patch of soft light across it from the porch lights mounted on the sides of the building. The chopper hovered. He searched the branches of his tree for specific shapes, but there was a breeze, perhaps from the helicopter, and the branches kept shifting before they could hold a picture. He shivered, the night was hot. His clock hummed. The chopper blades beat. His heart ticked.

The helicopter swung around, so the voice was faint at first, then louder, filling the summer night, right outside his window, coming from the sky, "We're looking for a lost elderly man, age around ninety-three, wearing brown trousers and a red plaid shirt and glasses. He's confused and wandering in this area. If you've seen this man, please contact . . ."

He shut his eyes when he thought he saw a face looking through the window, but it was the branches of his tree. The twigs tapped on the glass. He lay without moving, the voice of the chopper fainter, now farther away, ". . . confused and wandering . . . ," then the voice trailed away.

He moved back to his stepparents' house.

*I had gone to a travel agent and brought home brochures so I could plan a trip for Grandpa. Before I could decide where to go, Grandpa died.*

*I put the travel posters up in my bedroom and postponed the trip for a while.*

# 24

## ISOLATED INCIDENTS

They interviewed him before they would do any cutting.

Sterilization is a serious step, son, the doctor said.

I know enough to decide.

The doctor left the nurse to talk to him.

How old are you?

Twenty-four.

You see, sometimes when you're young, you make rash decisions which you regret ten years later. You can't reverse this decision when you realize you don't really mean it.

I know.

This will be forever.

I know.

To protect you, we're supposed to determine how convinced you are. He won't do it if we feel you're not convinced or haven't been informed about the finality of this decision.

I don't want children.

Do you have a reason, or are you just afraid of being tied down to a responsibility?

I don't mind responsibility.

Is your wife afraid of pregnancy, or does she have some medical problem which makes pregnancy dangerous for her?

I'm not married.

Don't you think this decision should be discussed with a spouse? What if you someday marry a girl who wants a family? Don't you think it would cause problems in your relationship if you were unable to fulfill her desire?

I'm not getting married.

How do you know that now?

I just know.

Suppose you did.

I won't.

Hypothetically.

She would know beforehand I can't have kids. If it bothers her, she can marry someone else.

What if you loved her?

It's got to be more profound than a whim to procreate.

Idealism like this is fine now, when you're young. You don't even realize that you could regret this.

How can I regret it.

What is your reason for not wanting children?

I've thought about how I would be allowed to pick their names and choose their clothes and decide what school they would go to and read books to them and teach them how to do what I know how to do. But beyond that, I can't control how they turn out.

You don't understand the strength of parental love because you haven't experienced it.

They could turn out to be dope dealers or fugitives or rapists or somebody nobody likes.

How would you like it if that was the attitude your father had?

I don't know who my father is.

She told him to shave his groin before he came back for his appointment.

He was lying on the table, naked, hairless like a baby, and the doctor said, I guess you'd make a pretty lousy father.

He applied anaesthetic and turned on the hot lights. Phelan thought his penis must be on fire.

A nurse came in. He remembered he was naked. The doctor introduced him to the nurse.

The incisions were short. A segment of each tube was cut away and tiny clips placed on the severed ends.

The doctor sewed him up.

Look, the doctor said, like spaghetti. He held the two pieces of tube.

No sex for two weeks, the nurse said.

You'll need to come back for a sperm count in about a month, the doctor said.

Try not to scratch, the nurse said.

You know, the doctor said, looking at the tubes, it's not easy to adopt children. An agency decides whether or not you're a good risk.

# 25

## WORKING AT HOME

You wanted to *prove* I could paint, Phelan, so you dug out an old set, *Maine Fisherman* and *Fish Story*. Never any uglier. The fisherman looks too much like an astronaut, but with a foolish smile, slicker and boots and deep-sea diver's bubble over his head, seaweed growing all over him, fishtails sticking from his pockets and the tops of his boots. But *Fish Story* is worse. A boy squatting in the sand, underwater, surrounded by smiling perch and flounder. He holds a starfish. There's a bubbling castle, like an aquarium. I told you what I thought of those paintings. But you said I'd liked the story well enough when it had helped me paint them. I didn't remember any such story, and said so.

So you told me again about the old man we found in an opening of a crosswalk tunnel under a busy street, maybe a freeway, you said, but you weren't sure because it wasn't in California. When he saw you, he said he'd been waiting for you. He was pretty old—his name was Arthur. You went through the crosswalk tunnel to the other side of the freeway. You came out at the beach, out on some bluffs over the water. Yeah, this is the story with the goddamn ocean. Then you looked over your shoulder and there was no freeway there, which prompted old Arthur to say it was good that no one had followed you. There was a pier, or a ramp, dead ahead, starting on the bluffs and sloping down toward the water at an angle. You couldn't see the end of it out over the water. There were also steps down to the beach, you said, so this old guy gave you a choice, deep-sea fishing or wait for the grunion on the beach. Except instead of waiting there with torches to ambush the grunion and take them, you said, the fish would come with caviar which, according to some agreement, would allow them to go back into the water unharmed.

You took the blank canvas off the easel and put *Fish Story* there, and you leaned *Maine Fisherman* against the legs of the easel. Then you held my hand, massaging it a little.

You said you chose deep-sea fishing, so down the pier you went, and the pier went right into the water. You and the old guy also went right into the water, with a bubble of air staying around your heads. You finally stepped off the end of the pier, which rested in the sand at the bottom of the ocean.

There were fish all around, you said, but what's-his-name — Arthur — said not to bother them; they were busy. He said your job was to build a hideout. So what you did first was build an underwater palace.

You also took the time to point out to me that you were able to jump up and do a triple somersault before you landed.

There was a fish corral in back of the palace, all the fish you wanted. They could swim in and out of the bars, but there were always plenty there. But this wasn't all Shangri-la — it seems there was someone looking for Arthur who would kill him if they found him. That's what you said that he told you.

Old Arthur, it seems, had stolen the family fortune in gold. You called it his future; he was going to build a fish ranch and needed capital. The plans were made: breeding corrals and scientific feeding for faster growth, creation of hybrids for high egg output and high fertilization percentages, hormone injections and night-lights, tube-feeding around the clock. He had, you said, spent his whole life planning his future. But the rest of his family wanted the fortune back, so you and he guarded that palace with a moat full of eels and things that live in the mud.

Then they found you. Probably, you said, because you hid the gold in some fish, by feeding it to them, and some of the fish were transparent and glowed. So they — whoever they were, you just called them *they* — surrounded the palace. They wore wet suits with flippers and masks and tanks. They didn't look like people at all, but of course, you and the old man still did, clothes and shoes and faces. *They* hovered around outside like long-legged black frogs. Old Arthur started to panic, but you asked if he recognized anyone out there. He said no, they were all so rubber-skinned. So your idea, you said, was maybe they wouldn't recognize him either if he stood near a window in his raincoat holding a pitchfork, prongs up. You told him he had a little stubble too, but he hadn't noticed it because you didn't have a mirror. Then you walked out over the drawbridge to talk to them, and they gathered around, their faces level with yours but their flippers floating up behind them. They fanned the water with their hands. You told them it wasn't their father. They looked at Arthur in the window, then back at you, nodding. One of them, you said, had glued his horn-rimmed glasses inside his mask. They didn't leave. One of them beckoned to Arthur to come out. You just repeated, it's not your father. You said you knew *their* father: a sweet old man watching his grandchildren grow, banging a frypan with a spoon on New Year's Eve, making sure there were enough shrimp in the spaghetti sauce, arguing with the produce man in the grocery store, handing out silver dollars he'd saved since the Great Depression to round-eyed grandchildren. Well this guy, you told them, pointing back at old Arthur — wearing his raincoat and holding a pitchfork — is a self-made business-man. He has no sons.

And that was the end. I guess the trick worked. You never said.

I asked, "Is that *all?*"

"All!" You jumped to your feet. Your legs couldn't stand still; you seemed to be dancing. "All!" You were laughing! Then you said, "Tara, make love with me."

We were already on our way to the bed. You were saying if I still believed I'd never made anything good or worthwhile, just look at you. I didn't understand and didn't ask because that's when I saw your penknife on the nightstand. I grabbed it and ran back to the easel. You were right behind me, but you didn't catch me before I stabbed that painting on the easel at least twice. When you caught me, we all went down together, the easel, the painting, you and me. I held onto the knife. You were on my back. I told you I hated it and I'd never painted it, but you said I just must've forgotten and it was okay. But dammit — if there's nothing to remember, there's nothing to forget.

I wonder what it would feel like to bleed from here. I remember once I told you: "I'm glad I don't menstruate."

You answered, "I wonder if maybe you should?"

"Why bother," I'd said.

I'll tell you what it feels like now: Like when you cleaned the fish your father used to catch, one finger back and forth in the slit between throat and grommet. And remember that grey corbina your father brought home from the beach, how he lay colorless strips of fillet on your hands for you to carry to the kitchen while he cleaned the knife and buried the guts. Then there were the cold feet of shelled abalone which your father pounded with a meat tenderizer but still took forever to chew.

# 26

## HOW TO LEAVE A COUNTRY

How long has he been gone, it doesn't matter, he'll feed himself when he's hungry and rest when he's tired. He's been on his own a long time now.

His mother thought he would starve when he went to Brazil. He hadn't gained weight since high school. He couldn't cook. But she didn't know about Anna; he was bringing Anna along. Anna had told him that they didn't need to get married because she would start birth-control pills. That was before his operation. (Mother didn't know about that either; he wasn't planning to tell her.) Then Anna had cried because *Consumer Reports* and medical studies tied the pill to cancer or any number of problems. So the operation made Anna happy since she wouldn't have to mess with diaphragms or pills or rubbers.

The important thing was Anna liked him.

She had been a typist in the art-department office and had said "Oh wow" once when she saw him wearing his favorite long-sleeved green shirt. Someone else had heard her and told him. So he asked her out and took her to a play where many of the actors knew him because he'd helped design the set.

Another important thing was his teaching job at the university down there. They wanted Americans to teach. A representative had posted a notice in the department office: Full professorships in the Arts and Sciences, Universidade do Estado do Rio de Janeiro, payment in American money.

He found Anna easier to convince than his mother.

"How much can I explain to her without hurting her feelings," he told Anna.

"Why so far away? Why Brazil?" his mother asked.

"It's not that I chose Brazil — I chose to leave."

"Buy why?"

"I can't be myself here."

"You've been yourself here for twenty-four years."

"She didn't understand," he told Anna.

"I don't think I do either."

"Sure you do. Listen: You're a secretary here, right? So suppose you wrote a book and it was published, would people around her think of you as Anna-the-author? No, you'd be Anna-the-secretary, who wrote a book."

"When will you come home?" his mother asked.

"I'll *visit,* but this won't be home."

"This will always be home."

"No, I've got to go somewhere, start over in my own place where I'll belong because it's *mine.*"

"Oh wow," Anna said.

"Yeah, she took it hard, she may've cried. It didn't come out the way I wanted."

"Did you tell her about me?"

"And open another can of worms?"

"Think of it this way," he told his mother, "I'm an artist now, and my own space is going to be my first and most important creation."

"Then why do you want me to come along?" Anna asked.

"How can you ask! You're part of it, because of the way you feel about me. . . . I'm not going to make the mistakes she did and fake it. Besides," he teased, "want me to be in love all by myself?"

Anna smiled faintly.

"Only two suitcases?" his mother exclaimed.

"Some new clothes I bought; all my tools."

"What about all your things?"

"I'm not leaving anything of mine here."

"I couldn't tell her how I feel here," he told Anna. "I don't think I can explain it—how a person can feel this way about a place they've lived . . . *eighteen* years. . . . She forgets when they gave me to her."

He held Anna's face with his fingertips. "An artist expresses love in his work, but he's still got to have it in his home first."

"How do people live down there?" his mother asked.

"Don't worry. I'll make it comfortable; it doesn't matter how they live down there."

Anna shook her head.

"Does it really sound silly?"

"Well . . ."

"That's the trouble with words—they don't do justice to a person's aspirations."

"You're young, son, I worry that you just don't know what you want."

"Dammit, Mom!"

"Can you forget the mushy way it sounds and come with me anyway?"

"Okay, sure. Anyway, I need a change of scenery."

He put his arm around her and she looked up at him. "You know the trouble with this?" she said. "Everyone secretly wishes corny things could be true, but they usually turn out to be bullshit."

Phelan laughed.

He found a large ground-floor apartment in Ipanema. Tiny kitchen, three bathrooms, living room, seven bedrooms and a walk-in storage closet. Anna said it was too big. "I'll never be able to keep it clean."

"I'll help," Phelan offered.

He was tired of looking at unsuitable locations, over factories or rock 'n' roll clubs, thick with roaches, one place where the neighbors raised chickens on the patio.

"This place'll work out perfectly" he told Anna.

Anna stood in the bathroom doorway tapping her foot, looking at the box on the wall. She didn't say anything about it, even after Phelan figured out it held the pilot light. When anyone wanted a shower, they lit the pilot and the bathroom water would heat up. The kitchen didn't have a pilot.

"Well, we can wash dishes in the bathroom if we want hot water," Phelan said.

One of the rooms was large enough to be a studio with morning-light windows. He built a workbench along two sides of the room, leaving the center free for larger statues to be worked on there, or a potter's wheel, if he had to resort to that for extra money. He set roach traps and hung flypaper. He sanded and repainted the ceiling in the studio, fearing the old paint would flake into his clay.

"You wouldn't want crap falling on us while we make love," he said to Anna.

"We're going to do that *here?*"

"Where else?"

"Maybe the bedroom?"

He smiled.

*It was always hot, making both the clay and me sweat. But the studio felt good. Many times I worked in my underwear. I prepared the raw materials: clay and water. I had a pillar of clay as tall as myself which I put on a small platform with wheels so I could have easy access to every side. The water helped keep the clay supple, to give me maximum control, but I didn't need to use it often because my own sweat kept my hands and tools damp and gave me all the control I needed.*

Each floor in the building was a separate apartment. All apart-
ments were connected by a single garbage chute, terminating
in the basement, the floor below Phelan. Sometimes the basement became too full and the trash would back up in the chute
and spill out into Phelan's kitchen if he opened the little door.
He would have to carry his garbage down to the basement
himself. Anna suggested he put it out on the sidewalk because
some bum might find something useful — like the American
magazines she bought for three times their cover price; and she
never chewed all the meat off her take-out chicken bones like
Phelan did. But Phelan wouldn't put the garbage on the street.
    Official paperwork started next. And continued.
    He tried to file his papers on his own, but angry clerks threw
his forms away and sent him to a *despechante,* a special lawyer
for legal documents. The lawyer smilingly explained it might
take years if Phelan tried to apply for his own documents,
whereas he knew the system. An ID card was essential, telling
nationality, age and sex. He couldn't get a paycheck without
one. And if a policeman wanted to know who he was but he
didn't have an ID, he would go to jail for not being able to prove
he existed.
    The *despechante* quoted a price and told Phelan to leave his
passport.

The bus trip out to the university took over an hour, but Phelan
used the time to study Portuguese. He took a class, three nights
a week, two and a half hours, repeating phrases, conjugating
verbs. Anna didn't take Portuguese lessons. Phelan had to
order for both of them at the restaurants every night. She didn't
know how to cook either. She didn't have a working visa, only
tourist papers, so she didn't get a job. He was worried about
her. He thought she might get bored and go home. He kept
suggesting hobbies; he bought her a set of paints and two small
canvases. She took them out to the beach and painted a bou-
quet of flowers. She got sand in all the paints and lost one of the

canvases on the beach, but Phelan put the flower painting up
in their bedroom over the bed. She went to the beach without
the paints from then on. She was always peeling a layer of skin.
She took up smoking. Phelan, worried that she wasn't happy,
would rush away from the university to spend time with her.
Sometimes in the afternoon he tried to convince her to make
love.

He spent the evenings alone in his studio.

Commuters boarded the bus at the back and could either sit
there and pay to get off at the front or pay first and sit at the
front, thus being allowed to exit the bus more quickly. The
turnstile was in the aisle near the middle of the bus where an
official took the bus fare then gave each passenger a plastic
chip. The chips came in various colors. Black was the rarest.
When leaving the bus at the front, passengers were supposed
to drop the chips in a box there, but no one cared if they did or
didn't. The newspaper said that in the span of one year, three-
fourths of all city buses had been involved in accidents.

The first person he added to the household was a samba band
drummer from the nightclub on the corner. He was an American too; his name was Tad; he was without shame. One afternoon Phelan watched Tad try to pick up every girl on the
beach, moving from one to the next, asking the time, asking
for matches. When he got to Anna, she sat up and stretched
and told him it was four o'clock, time to go home, and Tad
came along with them. Anna and Tad talked about the States.
Phelan suggested they go somewhere for dinner, but Tad said
he could cook. He fried a steak then used the grease to heat up
some canned corn. They had steak and corn again for breakfast, and Phelan added Tad's name to the mailbox. Phelan
made a little marquee, mounted on the wall above the mailbox, his and Anna's names on one line with an *and* in between,
and beneath that, on another line, Tad's name. He and Anna

had one room, Tad another. There were several more empty rooms.

He helped Tad get a job teaching music at the university. The Brazilians were delighted. They asked Phelan if he knew any more talented Americans.

The university had students in grades one through graduate and gave degrees through Ph.D. Quality was important. The poetry department was cancelled for a year because no one wrote any good poems. If it wasn't for the professional musicians hired to play in the university orchestra, the instrumental music department would've been dropped too because the Brazilian student musicians were lousy.

When Phelan went in swimming, the waves and currents took him down the beach — the longer he swam, the farther down the beach. So when he walked out of the water, Anna never seemed to be where he left her, sitting on the sand on her towel. Anna never went swimming. He walked slowly back to Anna, walking where the water came up to his ankles then receded, leaving him on slick sand. When the meek waves came in again, he kicked them, splashing arcs of water in front of himself as he walked.

Someone was taking pictures of him.

He saw her up on the dry sand, heard the click-whir of the motorized camera.

The photographer stayed parallel with him, and when the photographer was standing right next to Anna's towel, still taking pictures, Phelan turned away from the water and walked face-on into the camera.

The photographer, behind Anna, lowered the camera from her face, a little surprised, a little scared.

She was American too. Jan Marsh sat down on a corner of Anna's towel. Phelan sat in the sand and buried his legs. The sand was warm, almost hot.

Jan Marsh was skinny, without a figure. She said she'd come down to Rio to do a picture story for *Life* but had never been able to sell it, then had never left because she'd found so many things to shoot. "I get by on what I sell down here," she said.

"I'd like to see some of your work," Phelan said.

"Yes, I have a set of Brasilia showing the stark reality."

"Do you ever leave the city? I'll bet you could get some great surreal shots of insects and bugs here, huge butterflies, all those colored caterpillars. You could do a science-fiction set out in the jungle."

"You never want to go into the jungle," Anna said. "You've said so."

"I'm afraid of bugs, but I wouldn't mind seeing pictures of them. They have special lenses, you know, that can put you face-to-face with a bug and blow him up to human-size. Right, Jan?"

"A macro lens," Jan Marsh agreed.

She said she didn't have her own studio or darkroom, but had set up a makeshift area in her apartment. She couldn't stop all the light leaks, though. Phelan's house had a small room without windows: the walk-in storage closet made a perfect darkroom. He added her name to the marquee, JAN MARSH, PHOTOGRAPHER, on a separate line, below Tad. If she got together with Tad, he'd have to change it, but that was okay too. She put the photos of Phelan splashing water on the living room wall, five of them in a row. She named the set "Water Games" and tried to sell it to a few places, but she said it wasn't what her regular buyers wanted.

With four people now, the house had to be organized. Everyone got a shelf in the cupboard and in the refrigerator. Anna and Phelan shared, of course; they were a pair. He drew up a schedule and posted it in the kitchen, giving the stove to Tad at six, and to Jan Marsh at six-thirty, and to himself and Anna at seven. They took the late shift because they still ate in restaurants almost every night, unless Anna boiled spaghetti. A pad for messages was necessary next to the phone, and a Kaper-Chart for housecleaning chores. They swapped every week-end: Someone cleaned the bathrooms, someone else vacuumed, someone dusted.

The university was happy to have Jan Marsh teach photography. She had one or two students. A third showed up once a month, then dropped out. She was out doing photo sessions most nights, worked in her darkroom until dawn, slept, then went out to the university or the beach in the afternoon. She and Anna did not become friends, but they weren't enemies. She didn't become lovers with Tad either. Phelan encouraged Jan Marsh to market her photos at the best Brazilian magazines. She smiled and said "Okay."

Phelan made ceramic nameplates for the bedroom doors.

*I never considered it work. Sometimes it seemed I could tell the clay to take a new shape and it would, on its own, remembering each instruction. The possibilities were limitless, and every day the piece changed to something else—not anything I planned, sometimes something I hardly expected. Once or twice something human evolved. Many times it pleased or fascinated me—what I'd made of the clay that day—but I didn't hesitate to continue changing it, because although I felt good, I didn't feel good enough to call it finished. I had to feel more than good. At least I was satisfied with the progress, because I still had control over every shape it took, and the final thing would be utterly mine. I would know it when I had it.*

Out on the sidewalks, he had to watch where he was going, watch that he didn't step in someone's fire or on someone's sacrificial offering or on someone's leg; and watch out he didn't walk under someone's garbage as they threw it out the window; and make sure he didn't walk in the line of fire of someone who needed to spit a large glob of mucus out of a door or window, out of a car or bus; or any fellow pedestrian who at any moment might turn his head and spit over his shoulder. He almost stepped in the derby hat placed on the pavement on the corner near the bus stop, where two Americans, one freckled and red haired, were singing duets for Brazilian pennies — each cruziero bill that week worth five cents, each Brazilian centavo about .05% of a penny.

Phelan stopped to listen. They had operatic voices but sang American folk songs in Portuguese, the tunes the same, the words plugged in to fit the melody. Their accents were terrible. He couldn't understand the lyrics. The girl singer swung her ass and bumped hips with her partner, but he moved away, out of reach, and didn't gyrate at all as he sang. He was the freckled one. The girl was not light but not dark, not tall, not short, not all skinny or not all fat — her shoulders and chest tiny, pinched, hungry-looking, her ass big and soft — the classic pear shape, except this pear was half-eaten, nibbled on around the top so the stem came up naked out of the big bottom. Phelan emptied his pockets into the hat. The girl smiled and sang just to him until the end of the song. Then Phelan found out they were married, Danny Middleton and Cassandra Bolivar. "Call me Sandy," she said. She had brown-black hair, already flecked grey. Maybe twenty-six. Her husband looked twenty. He didn't say much, but he said it was true after Sandy told Phelan that they'd come down from New York, promised a place in the National Opera, but nobody down here had heard of them when they showed up. They picked up enough change daily to pay the hotel bill, but the roaches were as big as their hands, and the rats must be the size of cats, judging from their turds.

Everything had to be adjusted. Names added to the Kaper-Chart and kitchen schedule. There weren't enough chores, so Phelan fixed the chart to allow a free weekend for each of them the week before they were assigned to clean the bathrooms. With the change in the kitchen schedule, Anna and Phelan were up to eight o'clock. Anna tapped her foot about that, so

Phelan said each shift had a five-minute grace period. If they hadn't started cooking five minutes after their shift started, it would mean they were forfeiting the kitchen for the night, eating out or not hungry, and the next shift could start early.

Phelan bought more plastic letters for the marquee. Danny and Cassandra shared a line, an *and* between their names, like Phelan and Anna. He asked them if they wanted a *Mr. and Mrs.*, so it would show they were married, since Cassandra had kept her maiden name. Cassandra said, "No, that's okay. We know."

She reminded him to call her Sandy.

"You want *Sandy* on the marquee?"

"No, never!" she laughed. "Cassandra's my professional name."

But for their ceramic nameplate, for their bedroom door, Phelan made DANNY AND SANDY, because she should be Sandy there.

They weren't without jobs long. The university hired them for the vocal music department. Danny soon became department chairman, but Cassandra quit when she started singing with Tad's band, but that didn't happen until after Robyn Woo and Weird Bob moved in.

So far he hadn't needed to buy any more clay. He hadn't dried or fired anything.

After a symphony concert, Phelan suggested they wait for the musicians to come out so they could congratulate them. Anna looked at the taxi line, growing shorter as the concert hall emptied.

"Okay?" Phelan urged.

Anna nodded, yawning. "Somebody beat you to it," she said.

A slight blond man, his hair slicked back and darkened with oil, was speaking to the musicians as they came out the stage door. He repeated, "Americano, Americano," and tapped his chest as he stepped in front of each. A few of them muttered "Me too," but they also brushed past him or yanked their arms away when he tried to shake hands.

"Ah, Robyn!" the man exclaimed, seeing an Oriental woman. He took her hand and tried to take her cello as he led her to the sidewalk. They stood waiting for a cab near Phelan and Anna. The Oriental girl was trying to pull her hand away, saying "Forget it, shithead," in a Brooklyn accent.

"Endearments from home," the little man smiled. The girl looked for a cab.

"Do you know him?" Anna asked her.

"I know who he is," the girl answered. She didn't take her eyes off the street. She finally pried the man's hand off her sleeve.

"Where are you from?" Phelan asked him.

"Alabama."

"Can't you tell?" the girl said.

"What are you doing down here?" Phelan asked him.

"I needed to flex my imagination."

"One shitty place is the same as another," the girl said. "You can pretend that one's better or different . . . "

Anna had stopped yawning.

"Are you an artist?" Phelan asked the man.

"I don't draw pictures, if that's what you mean."

"Not enough cabs in this shitty city," the girl grumbled.

"Maybe we can share one," Anna offered. "Where do you live?"

"Are you a musician?" Phelan asked.

"Nope."

"Over a bar that's open all night," Robyn said.

"That's no place for a girl to live alone," the little man said.

"Shut the fuck up."

Phelan got a cab and they squeezed into the backseat, the cello lying across everyone's knees.

"You a poet?" Phelan asked the man.

"Naw."

"Any sort of writer?"

"Naw."

"An actor?"

"Nope."

"What do you do for a living?"

"Nothing right now."

Anna looked out the side window, humming a song that Sandy sometimes sang around the house.

"What are you good at?" Phelan asked.

"I don't know. Conversation. I can talk to anyone."

"That would be a good quality for an entertainer, like a comedian, or also a teacher."

"I'm not a comedian or a teacher."

"Everyone has some sort of talent," Phelan said.

"Yeah, I can type," Anna said, still looking out the window.

"I taught you to paint."

"Swell."

The cab ride was rough and dangerous, but they'd all lived there long enough to ignore it.

"Have you ever worked with your hands?" Phelan asked.

"Has he ever worked at all," Robyn said.

"I sold encyclopedias door-to-door."

"And you made enough money to get to Brazil?" Phelan asked.

"No. I got here by smuggling. There's a system. I brought in a suitcase full of stuff, then never claimed it after I got off the plane. My contact must've picked it up himself later. You hafta have a contact. He paid my way down here. I never met him, his contact contacted me when I lived in New York."

"There must be something you can do down here. Everyone can do something," Phelan said.

"Maybe I can," Weird Bob said.

"Where do you live?"

"With whoever will have him," Robyn said.

The cab bumped, swayed, swerved, squealed along without conversation for a while. Then Phelan said, "I have an idea for both of you."

The marquee read,

PHELAN BARKLAY AND ANNA SIVILS
TAD HUNTER
JAN MARSH, PHOTOGRAPHER
DANNY MIDDLETON AND CASSANDRA BOLIVAR
ROBYN WOO
WEIRD BOB

To make enough room, Phelan and Anna had to move their bed and clothes into the studio. He winked at her and she looked away. He kept his project covered with a wet cloth and asked Anna not to look under it. She shrugged and complained that the room smelled like dirt.

# 27

## WORKING AT HOME

Phelan, you swore to me: you *could* teach painting. You already had. I was your first failure. You didn't say that. I did, though. You shook me: No!

I shrugged. We were still on the floor. Pushed the paintings and easel aside. You took the knife. Side by side. On our backs. You held my hand again, holding it tight.

Damn — this is like scratching my ear when there's an itch in my head which I can't reach from the outside. Can't be reached from down here either. I've tried to use my hands like your sculpturing tools. The way you work — it doesn't look gentle or delicate. But this doesn't even hurt, not even pain.

You told me about a man who couldn't do anything, but *he* had learned to paint. Beautiful scenes, not copied — that's for sure — from anything, anywhere on earth. Painted with big hard calloused knobby hands. And I have these perfect ones. Perfectly useless.

No! You kneeled beside me. Shouted it. Your voice broke only once all day: Please don't do this to us.

I don't know why I ran.

Hey wait! You chased.

I was almost out the door and away. Almost got out of that damned studio.

You were so fucking strong. Hush, Tara, it's okay.

# 28

## HOW TO LEAVE A COUNTRY

While taking a walk, Phelan and Anna saw a construction crew tearing down a building. Two workers stood on a cement archway which spanned two sides of the structure, forty feet above the street, facing each other, pounding the concrete they were standing on with sledgehammers.

Every time he saw Jan Marsh, Phelan asked if she'd made any sales, and she smiled and said "A few," but she was too busy right then to show him or they hadn't been published yet. He asked Danny how Sandy was doing, but Danny usually said "I dunno," or "Ask her," or "Ask Tad." He asked Anna if Danny and Sandy were getting along okay. "How'm I supposed to know?" she said. She drank coffee all morning, until she went out to the beach.

"Well, I can't ask them," Phelan said, "and I just thought since you're here more than I am . . ."

"I see her around," Anna yawned.

He asked her if Robyn was making any friends.

"I dunno. Ask her, not me."

He asked Tad how the teaching was coming along and he asked Weird Bob when he could pay the rent. Then he finally saw Sandy again. He hadn't run into her after the first few weeks she'd been there. Their schedules conflicted. He'd heard she'd quit her teaching job. Anna had told him.

"I wanna go and hear Tad's band," Anna said. "He's got Sandy singing with him."

"What about Danny?"

"What about him?"

"He sings too."

"So?"

So when Phelan saw Sandy he asked about her new job.

"Oh yeah," she said. She was in a morning robe, looking much like a tepee. "Singin' samba."

"That's great, Sandy."

"Oh yeah — not Sandy anymore. What with the new job and all, I go by Cassie."

"Isn't Cassandra your professional name?"

"Cassie," she smiled. Some Brazilian dentist had filled the gaps between her teeth with yellowish cement. Her hair was gathered in a bun with wisps falling down in her face.

Phelan changed the marquee.

> PHELAN BARKLAY AND ANNA SIVILS
> TAD HUNTER
> JAN MARSH, PHOTOGRAPHER
> DANNY MIDDLETON AND CASSIE BOLIVAR
> ROBYN WOO
> WEIRD BOB

The ceramic nameplate on their door still said *Sandy.* She was probably, he thought, still Sandy there.

Everyone in the house rode a bus at least once a day. Anna and a few others, probably Tad and Cassie, started saving the plastic chips in a jar in the living room.

"You're supposed to drop those in the box," Phelan told Anna as she added a chip to the jar.

"We're saving them to play poker," she said. "The blacks will be ten-dollar chips. We only have one so far. Have you ever gotten one?"

"How are they gonna know how many people rode the bus if you don't give them your chips?"

"Who cares?" Anna turned the jar. "Mostly yellow so far."

Phelan washed the toilets every Saturday night when Anna went to hear Tad's band and most of the house was empty. He cleaned the bathrooms on both his and Anna's turns, according to the chart, and also on Tad's turn because the band was doing so well, working three or four nights a week plus rehearsals; for the same reason he took Cassie's turn too. He hadn't seen Jan Marsh for over a month. Her phone messages were still on the pad, other messages written over them. Robyn said she would vacuum twice but would not touch the toilets. He didn't trust Weird Bob to do it after Anna said he peed in the sink. Sunday afternoon was a perfect time to vacuum, everyone was out at the beach — everyone who had slept there. Then he worked in his studio. He hadn't thought of a title for his project yet. It would come to him when it felt right. He hadn't shown anyone.

Phelan said, "Whose phone message is this anyway, there's no name on it."

"Jan Marsh must be out on assignment," he said to Anna. She sat up and rubbed her eyes, then flopped over.

"Put some lotion on my shoulders, Phelan."

"Where do you want to eat tonight?"

"What day is it?"

"Wednesday."

"I'm eating at the club. I get to shake the maracas tonight for Tad."

A greasy frypan had been in the sink for a week. Phelan washed it and hung it up. He stuffed a few bags of trash into the chute. Anna blew on her fingernails. The red nail polish was the kind that glitters.

"You doing the maracas again tonight?" he asked.

"Nope. Only Wednesday. Friday is too busy."

He met Danny at school and asked him how he liked running
the department. "I petitioned for department chairman sta-
tus," he told Danny. Then he asked, "You still sing, don't
you?"

"In practice rooms," Danny said.

*One part of the figure I kept every day. It had been hard to
make, to give it enough support so it wouldn't fall. Maybe I
was proud of that technical success, but I think there was more
to it. It was an appendage that looped around the main body
several times without being attached, except where the appendage came out of the body.*

He got a letter from Jan Marsh in São Paolo. She would be back
in a week, maybe two or three. She'd enclosed the cover of a
magazine. He didn't know the name of it because the logo had
been cut off the top. The teasers printed in Portuguese on the
side were covered with tape except "New Photos by Marsha
Brighton." The cover photo was in black-and-white, a blank
white background and a black silhouette of a woman without
clothes standing with legs apart and stiff arms out to each side,
fingers spread. In her note, Jan Marsh said "photo by Jan
Marsh" made her sound like a lesbian so she was changing her
name. She hoped he liked her first important cover.

He adjusted the marquee.

PHELAN BARKLAY AND ANNA SIVILS
TAD HUNTER
MARSHA BRIGHTON, PHOTOGRAPHER
DANNY MIDDLETON AND CASSIE BOLIVAR
ROBYN WOO
WEIRD BOB

He also pried the ceramic nameplate off her door, then went
into his studio-bedroom and made a new one with her new
name to surprise her when she came back.

"Someone's an insomniac," he told Anna. "I hear them walking around at night."

"Tad and Cassie."

"What?"

"Coming home late from the club."

"They giggle a lot."

"Maybe they're happy." She put her cigarette out and rolled over.

Phelan said, "We'll have to get organized again."

The project stood covered with a damp sheet and a heavy cheesecloth.

The token official gave Phelan a blue chip.

"Save that," Anna said. "It's second best next to black."

Phelan dropped the chip into the box on his way off the bus.

"Oh you," Anna said and walked on ahead.

Weird Bob advertised an escort service for tourists but didn't have enough money for a personal phone. Girls often waited for him in the living room while he put on a clean tuxedo after his afternoon shift.

Phelan said, "I don't know whose dishes are whose anymore."

He put eight clips on the wall by the phone and labeled them with names, so phone messages could go to the proper person.

Marsha came back and called Phelan a sweetheart for making the new nameplate, then she spent three or four hours straight in the darkroom and forgot to show him the photos from the inside of that magazine.

Phelan waited up for Anna. "How were the maracas? Stay in tune?" He said it grinning.

"Very funny." She sat down and took her shoes off, then smoked a cigarette before removing the rest of her clothes.

"I saw Marsha leave for her photo session with Weird Bob tonight. She hire him to take her?"

"No," Anna said.

"I can't imagine Marsha and Bob actually dating."

"No. She went with him to meet his client."

"Looks like everyone's starting to do real well. I can take time out to do a bust of you, if you still want me to."

"No thanks."

He asked Tad if he was meeting any nice girls at the university.

"Can't talk now," Tad said. "Gotta run."

In the afternoon he still liked to tell Anna about his day, if she was there and not asleep.

"You've heard about losing something in the translation," he said. "Somehow I gained in the translation. It wasn't all that funny. I was telling them about a near miss on the bus this morning, how we came within a couple of feet of driving a taxi off a bridge. They all laughed too long. Maybe they think they have to treat me special because I'm American. I hope not. It makes me feel uncomfortable. Like a laugh track turned too high all the way through the dialogue of a show."

Anna was dabbing nail polish on a run in her nylons. She waited until he was finished talking. "I suppose you showed them how far away the taxi was with your hands measuring the distance."

"Of course."

"Well that one always means the size of someone's dick. In this case yours. Doncha think that's funny?"

On her way out she added, "And don't tell anyone they're doing fine by using that hand signal for okay. Here it means fuck-you. Okay?"

"Thanks. I'll remember that one."

The kitchen schedule fell off the wall and someone propped it up on the counter, but it got splattered with ketchup. Robyn still cooked at five and Phelan sometimes ate with her, but she never made more than one portion so he ate cheese sandwiches. He offered to do her dishes but she said no. She washed her own, then took out a clean towel every night to dry them.

She kept her dishes in her room, which left a bare spot in the dish cupboard for a while, but somebody started putting a saucepan there.

Sometimes Anna went to the movies with Phelan.

"Isn't that Danny up there in the front row?" he asked.

"Prob'ly." Anna chewed gum in theaters.

"Must be hard on him with Cassie singing nights. We should have asked him to come with us."

"Cassie ain't singing tonight. The band's off."

Phelan leaned forward and squinted. "I don't see her with him."

"She isn't."

"That's funny." He scratched his ear. Anna went for popcorn then came back.

"They're splittin'," she said.

The movie was *The Good, The Bad and The Ugly,* translated into Portuguese for the Brazilians, *Three Men in Conflict.*

Phelan went to the kitchen to eat with Robyn at five but found her already washing her dishes. She smiled shyly at him.

Anna told him she thought Robyn was falling for him.

"I think she really likes you," Anna said.

"What makes you think so?"

"She mentioned the other day she thought she'd give it a try to see what it's like."

"What what's like?"

"Oh, love and all that shit."

"But she didn't say *me.*"

"Who else?"

"Tad?"

Anna shook her head.

Cassie giggled when she told Phelan she was moving in with Tad. Phelan fixed the marquee.

PHELAN BARKLAY AND ANNA SIVILS
TAD HUNTER AND CASSIE BOLIVAR
MARSHA BRIGHTON, PHOTOGRAPHER
DANNY MIDDLETON
ROBYN WOO
WEIRD BOB

"What should I do about Robyn, talk to her about it?"

"Naw, she's harmless," Anna said.

One of the newspapers reported an incident at a road construction site where the foreman told a worker to redirect the traffic around the area while they were working. The worker picked up a brick and threw it through the windshield of an oncoming car.

Phelan had to use a snake in one bathroom drain after Cassie cut her hair and used some dye to make it solid black. For two days water had stood in the sink, and Anna caught Weird Bob peeing into that. "It's a stinking mess now," she told Phelan, so he stopped working on the new nameplate for Tad and Cassie's door and fixed the drain.

Phelan said, "We need to take a head count. Who missed the rent this month?"

He found a green bus chip in the washing machine when he took the laundry out.

"You really should put the chips in the box," he said to Anna as he hung her clothes in the closet.

"Wait, I need that blouse tonight, don't put it away."

Weird Bob announced his new job as a talent scout.

"You really get jobs for people?" Phelan asked.

"For girls, as models. With Marsha."

"With a name like Weird Bob, you know the type to trust him with their career," Anna said. She brushed cigarette ash off her sleeve. "There's so much dust in this room, Phelan, can't you keep your self portrait, or whatever this thing is, somewhere else?"

Phelan was tightening a small vise attached to his work-bench. It held Danny's nameplate in its jaws and Phelan snapped the *and Sandy* away from the *Danny*.

"She never said she was paying salaries," Anna said.

Phelan went out to the mailbox.

PHELAN BARKLAY AND ANNA SIVILS
TAD HUNTER AND CASSIE BOLIVAR
MARSHA BRIGHTON, PHOTOGRAPHER
WEIRD BOB, TALENT SCOUT
DANNY MIDDLETON
ROBYN WOO

He rolled to Anna's side of the bed and slept there. She was in the kitchen smoking and drinking coffee in the morning. Somebody's corn flakes weren't put away. She poured him a bowl of them.

"They're not ours."

"Tad won't mind. *Bon appétit.*"

She went to get dressed and Phelan washed all the dishes in the sink.

He had an appointment with the president of the university and a few other officials to discuss department chairman sta-tus. Before that he made a date with another teacher who wanted him to translate a letter into English. The teacher was forty-five minutes late. He couldn't understand why Phelan was anxious. He looked at Phelan as if he were crazy. Phelan said, "Just give me the letter and I'll translate it tonight." He was a half hour late for his meeting with the president. He stood panting in the outer office, and the secretary told him he was the first one to arrive.

He asked Anna if she was liking Brazil more, now that she was used to it.

She smiled. "Yes."

He squeezed her hand.

Teenagers came out to the beach after school. Weird Bob talked to them. They liked blond hair, so they listened. Anna lowered a strap and looked at her sunburn.

"I see Bob's drumming up business," Phelan said.

"I wonder how much commission he makes." Anna lowered her other strap also.

"You want him to get you a job?"

"Maybe."

"Maracas going out of style, or not enough money in it?"

"Shut up."

Phelan hugged his pillow at night. He still hadn't shown anyone his project.

In the morning Anna came into the studio in her pajamas and woke him. "The toilet won't work. I think somebody flushed a Kotex."

Phelan rolled over and looked at her.

A plunger fixed the toilet. Phelan and Danny usually took the bus to the university together. They never spoke of Sandy. Then Danny said, "You know, Sandy got a two-week gig in São Paulo. Pop stuff. I mean, Cassie."

Phelan said, "We have to get back on schedule, everyone's confused."


He watched Anna dig through a drawer. "Aha!" She found her lipstick. "And looky here!" She found two red chips at the bottom of the drawer.

"I wish you would put those in the box on the bus," Phelan said.

Anna held a mirror to apply her makeup.

"Did you drop by the *despechante?*" Phelan asked.

"I said I would. He says three more weeks at least. Also he had to up the price."

"Why?" Phelan tried to pick up the red chips, but Anna put them into her jeans pocket. "I'm getting nervous walking around without that card."

"Tad says it means he's having to bribe someone, so naturally he's got to charge you for the price of the bribes."

The kitchen smelled like something was burning. Phelan and Tad said hi to each other. Someone had thrown the kitchen schedule away after spilling hot grease on it. Tad must've borrowed Robyn's dinner time so he could get to the club earlier. Anna was smiling in the studio as she rolled panty hose up her legs. Phelan sat on the bed beside her. "Maybe Bob will book you for an exclusive engagement in my studio."

Anna stood up and adjusted her half-slip. "Too late."

*Damn! Sometimes, working on my project, I actually felt weak kneed with that sweet pain of an adrenalin rush, the way falling in love is supposed to feel. I thought maybe it meant that it was going to be better than I'd ever imagined when I finally finished.*

*I started seeing more specific images in it as I worked. I thought it might be the king of my own life-sized chess set, and I would go on to make all the other pieces too. It was a little too female, but it didn't matter. I've played with sets where I couldn't tell the difference and inevitably end up using the queen for the king. I did, however, quickly discard the title "King" as soon as it entered my mind. I briefly considered "Checkmate" or "Perpetual Check." I was afraid of anything corny, but in my mind I started calling it "The Ultimate Embrace."*

He was hungry at Marsha's dinner time, and couldn't wait the five-minute grace period, so he knocked on her door.

"Enter."

There were photos drying on a line: Anna's spread legs and the back of Tad's curly hair. Anna's head back, chin up, neck tight, like a rope.

"Okay, yes, I did it," Anna said. "You never went back to the doctor for a sperm count. I can't risk getting a baby."

He took off his pants and got into bed. Anna stood there. She picked up her nightgown. "And since you wouldn't ever do what Tad does to me . . ." She took her cigarettes from the nightstand. "Cassie won't be back for another month. They extended her contract." She picked up his pants from the floor and draped them over a chair. "The university called today. They can't give you department chairman status and pay if you're the only teacher in the department."

He jumped out of bed and started stabbing at his project with a ceramics knife, cutting right through the cheesecloth. "I run that department, I made it, I run it, it's mine, I made it — "

"I'll see you tomorrow, Phelan." She closed the door. He gouged gaping holes in the twisted mass of clay.

> PHELAN BARKLAY
> TAD HUNTER & CASSIE BOLIVAR & ANNA SIVILS
> MARSHA BRIGHTON, PHOTOGRAPHER
> WEIRD BOB, TALENT SCOUT
> DANNY MIDDLETON
> ROBYN WOO

Who the hell knew what it would say when Cassie came back.

# 29

## LION HUNTING

For a while he follows the dry creek bed instead of the trail. He watches his feet and picks his way along carefully. He never went back for his shoes.

When he feels the pinprick on his arm, he looks down and sees a mosquito attached to the inside of his elbow. He grabs his upper arm with his other hand and squeezes, applying pressure to the large vein with his thumb. It doesn't take too long. Noiselessly the mosquito bursts apart leaving a thin splatter of blood along Phelan's arm.

Another mosquito hums near his ear and several more hover in front of his eyes. He waves his arms angrily and leaves the creek bed, starting barefoot up the side of the hill. Before each step he analyzes the ground where his foot will go, bending over to look closer.

*I probably look like I'm looking for something. Am I, besides wasps and snakes? I have to start thinking of what to do. Have I been thinking about it? I thought chess is supposed to improve concentration.*

It takes a long time to get to the top of this hill. By the time he does, the sun is just about ready to appear. He turns around and looks back, half expecting to see a fire or explosion in the valley near the base of the hills.

*Like standing, alone, outside a kiln while inside a piece of sculpture blows up into a thousand unrecognizable pieces. What else can I do? I obviously didn't make it well enough in the first place.*

On another hill, still farther ahead of him, he can see the five pine trees again. He hesitates only a moment, then begins picking his way down the side of this hill and up again toward the flat place where the trees grow.

He'd brought a cousin up here once, when relatives visited and told the children to go play together. All she wanted to do was braid long strands of grass, while he was trying to show her how to scoop ant lions out of the sand and watch them rebuild their homes in paper cups or cardboard boxes.

He sits on the pine needles, spreads his legs in a V in front of himself and clears away all the needles between his legs.

*The mature player controls the board. When there's a lot of tension, he controls it so it's in his favor. When there's a rash of exchanges, he controls the outcome. Even when faced with forcing moves, he'll manipulate them into working for him. Listen to me, I can recite the theory but when have I applied it?*

He brushes the sand smooth and draws a chessboard with his finger.

# 30

## HOW TO LEAVE A COUNTRY

He was alone, his studio gloomy on a sunny Saturday afternoon. He looked down at the swollen phallus he was holding, and at his fist with its grey, chapped knuckles, slightly skinned and rough, as though he'd been fighting bare-handed. His movement was like that of scouring clothes on a washboard . . . better still, like using the plunger on the sink or in the toilet: Grip solidly, work up and down, hard as you can, until something breaks — you'll know it. You'll be finished.

One hand flying, flailing, paddling air, then during the inevitable spasm, he pounded on the clay thing standing in his studio, beside the bed.

He had already smashed the ceramic nameplate on the studio door — that morning, with a hammer. Not even bothering to take it off the door, he kept pounding until every piece of the Anna was chipped away, the Phelan part broken in two and filled with hairline cracks. He took the two halves of his name into the studio, clamped them in the vise and glued them together. He picked up all the Anna pieces, squatting in the hall for several minutes, picking up every crumb with his thumb and finger. He didn't know what to do with the handful.

Unglazed dry clay could always be returned to a bin of bits and pieces which he could soften with water and turn back into pliable material. But the Anna was glazed and baked. He couldn't return it to its original form.

He emptied the fragments into a pile on his work table, swept them into a mound with his fingers and dusted his hands, making sure none of the dirt fell onto the floor.

He didn't wash his hands before taking his penis out.

His shoulders felt tired and his neck stiff. He tried to shrug the feeling away, then gave up.

The house was quiet. He went barefoot into the kitchen. There was one banana left on the bunch he'd bought two days ago — one banana, a bruised one, and five or six broken-off stems. He just looked at the ravished bunch of bananas, then peeled the last one and stuffed it all into his mouth at once. He wandered into the living room.

That was where Robyn was reading an American magazine, not lying on the couch but sitting upright with crossed legs, wearing Brazilian jeans.

Phelan stood with a mouthful of banana. Robyn didn't look up. He chewed and swallowed, chewed and swallowed, chewed and swallowed. Then he said, "I thought nobody else was here."

"I didn't," she answered.

She looked up, but continued holding the magazine in reading position.

Someone walked across the living room on the floor above, thumping on Phelan's ceiling. He could hear himself breathing, but he wasn't panting. He realized that he had yelled when he ejaculated, not long ago. He shrugged again and wiped his hands on the butt of his pants, looking at his rather white, fairly long, very bony feet.

Robyn turned a page and said, "There's a concert you might like this week. Finally."

"Is there?" His voice was low and hoarse. He sat in an arm-chair he'd bought for the equivalent of five dollars.

"Yeah. A cello solo." She took her straight black hair from behind her ear and let it fall like a curtain over the side of her face.

"I don't know if I'll feel like doing anything," he said.

After the concert, Phelan waited at the stage door for Robyn. He took the cello and helped her into a cab. She wouldn't talk on the way back; she placed a finger across her lips and indi-cated the cab driver with her thumb. Phelan looked out the window, letting his neck and head bob like a wire doll with the rough movement of the cab. When they made a sharp turn, he fell sideways into Robyn. She pushed him away.

The first thing she said was "No one's home," before they'd even gotten to the door.

"How do you know?"

She smiled, twirling some hair around her finger. She pulled the hair across her face, under her nose, like a mustache.

When he stopped outside to straighten a few letters on the marquee, she went to her room, then was in the living room, in jeans, waiting for him.

"So, how'd you like the concert?" Robyn was on the couch. There was no room for Phelan there because she'd stretched her cello out beside her. Phelan sat in the chair.

"I can't remember what I was going to say in the cab. . . . What was it — were you trying to make sure he didn't take the long way home?"

"Those guys will listen in on personal conversations. It's the only way they can live through their shitty lives."

Phelan lounged back in the chair, his body like a ribbon fitting all the contours of the too-soft stuffed cushions.

"Well?" Robyn said.

"I don't know. Well what?"

"The concert — what'd you think?"

"Oh." He let his head tip back against the chair so he was facing the ceiling.

"Didn't you have a reaction? Where's your mind — you have one of *those*, don't you?"

"I can't decide — I mean, what I thought . . . wait a minute, it'll come to me — "

"What're you mumbling about over there? If you hated it, say so; if you just *praise* everything, there's nothing to talk about anyway."

"What? Oh . . ." What was that thing he'd said to Anna once, coming into the lobby at intermission. "Uh . . . Oh, I liked the soloist's attitude, the way he seemed to be talking to the orchestra with his music and listening as the orchestra answered."

Robyn turned off the lamp beside the couch. "If you only knew the real story," she said.

Phelan drummed his fingers on the arms of the chair.

"If you're not interested . . ." Robyn said, her voice fading in and out, her mouth dark in her shadowy face. "If you want to keep fuzzing-out, avoiding reality and believing the world is a beautiful place . . ."

Phelan waited. "No."

"Okay — that cellist, he wanted to be on a riser, higher than the orchestra, and he wanted the string section reduced, cut about in half, and he wanted the winds to hardly play. He wanted a real *soft* accompaniment because the solo isn't all that loud, and he was partly right because our conductor has tendencies to want the accompaniment too loud. But face it, most of it was his prima donna head. Anyway, the conductor refused to do any of those things. In fact, he encouraged the trumpets and trombones to play almost on the edge of distortion, certainly enough to drown out the solo, and he *added* strings and put most of the orchestra on risers — tonight was the first time we used those. That soloist retaliated against the retaliation and played badly on purpose tonight, couldn't you hear him squeak and garble up some runs? If there was a musical conversation between us and him, he was saying: I hate you shitheads; and we were answering: Prima donna cocksucker." Robyn chuckled a little, a weird sound following her voice from out of her dark corner. He'd never heard her laugh before.

"I understand . . ." his voice like a poor recording, ". . . when maybe he felt that what he was doing was worthless but he didn't know what else to try, why not stand up and yell *bullshit* at the audience. Or at the orchestra. At everyone."

She giggled, slightly snorting. "Sometimes I'd like to do that."

He waited. The silence was hot and still around them, and smelled sour. "I don't know . . . maybe smashing his cello on stage would've been a better communication. I don't know . . . who knows . . . some people can only backpedal and get farther and farther away. What did he want . . . ? What did he get . . . ?"

"His own goddamn way, and exactly what he deserved." He could hear her leg swinging rhythmically.

"I guess that's true. I don't care. I may've dozed off. Who knows. I wasn't paying that much attention, actually. I shouldn't tell you. I don't know why I am . . ."

"I don't blame you! He played like a dirge."

"How do you say 'I hate you shitheads' like a dirge?"

"He managed."

"Maybe mourning the fact that it's all he had to say."

"You're a real zombie tonight, Phelan. What've you been doing with yourself lately?"

"I've been to school and back. Every day."

"Big deal. What else?"

"Nothing. What else is there?"

"Perfect!" Robyn's voice leaped, no longer the bored, nasal sound. "It's so good to hear someone else say that! *The* question! You know, you're probably just like me. We're a good pair."

He blinked. He could see her eyes, dark and yet shining. He could see her mouth moving quickly. He couldn't see much more.

"Yes!" She laughed a little. "You know, I've been thinking a lot about that very thing, and so . . . well, I've been wondering what affairs are really like."

Phelan listened, then sat listening to it over again in his head. Finally he said, "Huh?"

"What you said — I've been thinking the same thing, and if I've been wondering what I've been missing, maybe I ought to try it."

Silence didn't make the room any darker. Finally he said, "What are we talking about?"

"Listen, everything is logical if you're aware enough. First, people have to stop fuzzing-out, you know, stop avoiding the severe facts-of-life. *I've* faced life and it's pretty shitty. So when you're aware enough to know something's missing, you're ready! Everybody seems to want to have affairs. Can they *all* be wrong?"

"Why are we talking about affairs?" Phelan said.

"You're so coy. I like that."

"Huh?"

"Well, after all, you're experienced and I'm not."

"At what?"

"Affairs and shit."

"I haven't had an affair."

"Yeah, of *course* not, Anna was just . . . you know . . ."

"I didn't have an *affair* with Anna, we were — "

"Anyway, lately I've been wondering what affairs are really like, and — hey, I know, maybe I'll have one!" Robyn laughed. She must not have heard Phelan say, "An affair is different than a relationship. . . ."

"Come on," Robyn said, "Let's plan my perfect affair. Anything goes, come on, let's plan." She put the cello on the floor and stretched out on the couch, her hands under her head. "A brand new experience . . . let's see . . . who'll it be. . . ?"

"Why don't you just wait and see?" Phelan said. "I mean, someday maybe someone will—"

"Plan in advance and you'll know what to expect. Come on, help me plan what to expect. . . ."

He looked down at his hands. "A mysterious stranger—"

"No, someone lonesome and in need, desperate, mournful, sensitive, gentle."

"Doesn't sound like much of a lover."

She looked at him, a light from outside showing in her eyes. "My insatiable lover. He'll be perfect. Now for the setting . . ."

"Outdoors," Phelan offered. "On a deserted beach."

"No, wait. I've got it—in someone else's house! So nothing is familiar, neither one stays, neither one comes and goes."

"Like an abandoned cabin."

"Or just an apartment. We'll break in when no one's home, finish and leave before they get back, straighten up and they'll never know."

"And pretend it never happened," Phelan mumbled.

Robyn stopped for a moment, then went on, "And he'll be insatiable, no time to take his clothes off, his desire is urgent."

"It's a cheap novel," Phelan said.

"No." Robyn's voice was unchanged, coming from her dark face. "He'll be patient too, understanding. He won't think it's weird that I've never done this. He'll want me, a deep want, and he'll keep going, all night." Her voice stopped. Then she added, "Yes, all night if necessary." She shifted her weight; Phelan couldn't see if she changed positions. "Kind of vague, huh?" she said.

"Yeah."

"So what does it need? Nothing kinky."

"How about what he looks like?"

"Doesn't matter. It'll be too dark to see. What else?"

"How about where you'll live . . . a Pacific island? Greenland? Capri?"

"No, I told you we'll borrow an apartment—neutral territory."

"Oh, neutral . . . not hostile, not . . . whatever." He paused. "Well, it doesn't sound like much of a story. I don't know. I don't think it'll sell, Robyn, even if you put a naked lady on the cover."

"No one's naked," she said quickly. Phelan yawned, tried to check his watch but it was too dark and his dial wasn't luminous. "So, you wanna add some details?" she said.

"I don't think we can be coauthors. You don't like my ideas."

"Well, after all, it's *my* affair. I'm just offering to let you help."

"I don't feel much like arguing," Phelan said. She didn't answer.

Cars went by. He started to count them, then got lost. He stared at his hands, curled, motionless in his lap. He recognized the sound of a bus. The signal changed and motors idled.

Robyn said, "Something went wrong."

"Sorry."

"So'm I, . . . but . . . it's not too late . . . is it? We *could,* you know, start over . . . couldn't we?"

Phelan looked up. He rose slightly in his chair, sat up straighter. His eyes had adjusted to the dark. He could see Robyn. Her black hair and pale skin. Her small, heart-shaped mouth. He wet his lips. "Yes . . . I suppose . . . we could." The cars moved on, and when the street was fairly quiet again, he said, "We should do that." He stood.

"Not here." Robyn also stood but left her cello on the floor. "Come on."

He followed her down the hall, even darker than the living room. He turned the light on when he passed the switch, but she whirled and said, "No!" He saw her face, panicked, in the flash before he turned the light back out.

She opened Tad and Cassie's door without knocking.

"What're you doing?" He wasn't sure why he was whispering.

"It's okay. He's out with Anna and Danny. Come on."

"But what—" He looked at her. She still held the doorknob, standing aside for him to go in first. "Do you think we should do this?" he asked.

"I *said* it's okay." She went on into the room, but he remained in the doorway.

"No, I mean . . ." He paused, looking at her. Then he looked away. ". . . is *this* really what we should do . . . as a beginning?"

"How else is there to start except starting?"

"It just seems . . ." His head down, he only saw her from her knees to her feet.

"Do you have a better idea?" she snapped. She lay on the bed. A streetlamp outside made visible the rose-colored bedspread—actually faded brown—pulled over unmade sheets.

He looked at her again. "I always thought . . ." He put one hand on the back of his neck and massaged that stiff place. "But what difference does that make." He shut his eyes briefly. "Anything's worth a try, I guess." He put his hands in his pockets and slouched a little.

"Good. Now that's settled." Robyn reached over her head with one hand, found the cord for the curtains without looking, without fumbling, and pulled them shut.

"You act like you've been here before," Phelan said.

"Only when no one's home." She spoke a little louder.

Some of the light was cut out, but the curtains were threadbare. He walked to the side of the bed.

"You can start," she said.

She lay spread-eagled, as though tied to the bedposts. But there weren't any bedposts; Tad had just a mattress and frame, and lucky to have that. Someone had left it behind when she moved out of his last apartment.

Phelan said, "Just a sec." He went out of the room and out the front door and changed the marquee. He put Robyn's name up next to his.

She hadn't moved. "You didn't need to lock the house. No one'll be home tonight. You didn't think I'd be stupid enough to not make sure of *that* first, did you? Thoughtful of you to consider my reputation, though."

"Huh?" He was pulling his pants off over his feet.

"What're you doing!" She bolted upright. "No, goddammit."

He stood holding his pants. "Huh?"

"Put them back on."

He started unbuttoning his shirt with one hand.

"No. I said no."

Neither one moved. Cars honked. A taxi's brakes screamed.

"No," Robyn said.

Phelan pulled his pants back on but left them unzipped. He also left his shirt unbuttoned and didn't put his shoes back on either. Robyn lay down again, then edged over to one side and Phelan lay down beside her. He said, "I understand. Don't worry." He propped himself on his side, leaning on his elbow, facing her. "I wonder if I'm getting old. I feel so stiff and achy."

She put her hands under her head. The light was gauzy and the room musty. His own room was damp and earthy, but this one was stale. He passed his free hand lightly down her body, starting with just his fingertips on her neck, then down over her shirt collar and shoulder, down along the side of her ribs, down to her belt and jeans. He let his hand rest on her hip a moment, then moved it across the front of her jeans, across the buckle and button-up fly, to her other hip.

"Take me," she said. He looked at her belt buckle. She rolled to her side, face-to-face with him, body-to-body, chests, stomachs, hips and knees. They were the same height. She gripped him, then rolled again onto her back, taking him with her. He lay on top. She moved her hips against him, so he also began rubbing against her, then she stopped moving. He slowed too but she said "Don't stop," so he continued humping against her. But with his pants unzipped, only his underwear was between her sharp belt buckle and his penis. He sat up, straddling her. When he stopped moving, she started again. "Oh yes," she said. Her eyes were closed. She rubbed her belt buckle against his nuts.

"Robyn," he said.

She stopped moving and opened her eyes. "What?" Her voice was flat.

"What do you suppose would *happen* if you took off your jeans?"

"No."

"Why not?"

"Not that, dammit."

"Why?" He leaned forward, perhaps to kiss her, but she turned her face away. "What are you afraid would happen? He was up on hands and knees, hovering over her.

"I'll get pregnant."

Phelan laughed, but gently. Robyn crossed her arms, still looking away.

"No," he said, "you won't." He waited for her to look at him. "I promise," he said. She still wouldn't look, so he used a finger to turn her head. Her eyes were dry. "Listen," he said, "don't worry. I don't work that way."

"I don't either."

"No, I mean I'm fixed, I can't have kids."

"Well, *I* can."

"You don't understand —"

"Neither do you."

"Come on, I promise, you'll see." He sat up.

"No, I don't need to take them off."

He sighed, looked down at her jeans, then back at her face. Her skin was like a mask with eye holes, nostrils and mouth cut out, blinking up at him.

"How about the belt?" he said.

"No."

They sat that way for a while, Phelan looking down at his crotch: his pants unzipped to show a V of white underwear, and her belt buckle pressed up against his nuts.

"Are you going to leave me?" she said. Her voice small.

After a moment he said, "What do you want me to do?"

"Do what you were doing. She closed her eyes and appeared asleep. He moved one knee between her legs and lay down on her again, so this time he was humping one of her thighs. It was smoother, at least, no bones or buckles. She had a little change in her pocket, though.

This position put his face down against her collarbone, which was rather prominent. She still wasn't moving by herself, but his movement pushed his thigh up between her legs. She didn't really moan; she said "Ah," frequently and distinctly. He was staying hard. Then she said, "You're too heavy. It's too hot." So he had to prop himself up with his arms in order to go on. He didn't look at her face. He hung his head and looked down her shirt front to their crotches rubbing on each other's thighs, an upside-down view of the activity.

When his arms got tired, he lay down again, but this time with his torso on the bed beside her, their legs still scissored together, humping. Propped up on one arm, he put his other hand on her belly.

She turned and opened her eyes to look at him. He smiled. His deft fingers undid her lowest shirt button.

"No."

He undid another button.

"No." She caught his wrist. The humping slowed and stopped.

"Why?"

"Not yet."

She had a strong hand. She held just his wrist. With his long fingers, he could've managed another button or two, but he didn't try.

"There's something I have to find out first."

"What?"

"How much I like this."

"Seems like you do."

"But do I like it enough?"

Even though she lay on her back and he on one side beside her, his top leg was still half across her, her legs wrapped around it like a pole.

"How'm *I* supposed to tell you that?"

"By making sure I do."

"I'm trying —"

"Help me," Robyn said.

"Okay, but —"

"It's *my* fucking affair."

He didn't say anything. It was quite late, one or two in the morning. He started to go soft. He moved his crotch up tight against her hip. She was still holding his wrist.

She said, "When I was little, my older sister used to make me bump asses with her. When we were both naked, after a bath or something, she'd say, 'Let's bump bottoms,' and I'd have to do it. She made me stand back to back with her, and then we both bent over and our asses touched. I hated it because I never knew when our cold asses would touch 'cause I couldn't see, of of course. I like to know what to expect."

"Okay . . ." Phelan looked down at his bare chest. His shirt was pulled off his shoulders, down his back, but the sleeves were still on his arms. He said, "May I take my shirt off?"

"No."

"Please — it's twisted and uncomfortable."

"No it isn't."

"Yes — I can hardly move my arms."

"Oh. I thought you said 'Can I take *your* shirt off.'"

"Oh."

"Okay, go ahead," she said. "Just your shirt." She let go of his wrist and he wiggled out of his sleeves. Then she caught his wrist again.

"See, it's not too cold," he smiled. She didn't smile back.

"It's important to me," she said, "that this is done right."

"I agree."

One of Phelan's hands was propping his head up, the other was being held at the wrist by Robyn. So she was the only one with a free hand. She didn't unbutton her shirt, but she did pull it up. She wore no bra. She bunched the shirt up under her chin and armpits.

He looked at her face.

"Look at me," she instructed.

"What?"

"Am I deformed?"

He stared at her — at her face.

"Look," she directed.

"Oh." He glanced down her torso. "No, you're not deformed."

"I want the truth."

"That's it." He didn't look down at her body again, but he began moving closer, to put their bare chests together.

"No," she said. She pulled her shirt down. "Do what you did before." She released his wrist and once again put her hands under her head.

He didn't move for a minute, propped up above her but not touching her except where his crotch was pressed against her bony hip. Then he did begin to move, slowly at first, then quicker, and also harder, digging a well while growing more thirsty, each push heavier. Then he began to grunt in his chest with each thrust, the shovel giving way to a pick then to a sledgehammer, but his penis never hardened again. As the work became heavier, he continued to accelerate, his rhythmic grunt nearly a shout, nearly a word. He stared at her face without blinking, until he thought he couldn't go faster and couldn't push harder, but he did, grinding his soft, uninvolved penis against her pelvic bone, watching as she began to pant and writhe, gasp and cry out, over and over, holding his wrist with one hand, beating the mattress beside herself with her other fist. She exclaimed, "My god, you're insatiable!" Then her gasps, squeals and cries started again.

At last Robyn lay still, flattened on the bed. She let go of his wrist. He released her, stopped moving, lay on his back beside her, staring at the cobwebbed ceiling.

Robyn said, "Whew!"

Phelan turned his head, facing her profile. "Hey," he said.

She didn't face him, but said, "What?" She had an odd smile, which began to fade.

"Please, let's start over again, maybe tonight . . ."

"What for?"

"We can make it better. . . Let me try. We didn't really . . . well . . . make love. . . ."

"No, we're not going to fuck. I never intended to. Dammit, what the hell do people want, anyway—isn't anything ever enough?"

It was finally dawn. "I think I'll sleep a few hours, then get up for my morning rehearsal," Robyn said. "Goddam orchestra won't give me a moment's rest." She stretched. She didn't even have to put her shoes back on because she'd never taken them off. She looked both ways out the door, then went down the hall to her own room.

Phelan lay there staring, reached into his underwear and fingered himself until he was hard, then zipped his pants up, snug over the erection.

The phone rang but he didn't answer it. Maybe Robyn did. He ain't home, Phelan said. Or he may've said it. He wasn't sure. He was too far away, too far to hear or even see his lips move. Far, far away, this building, this street, this city, a spot on the map.

He took his shirt and shoes, threw them into his studio on his way out the front door. He stood there barefoot and half naked and picked the letters of his own name off the marquee, off the line next to Robyn, and put them into his pocket.

# 31

## HOW TO LEAVE A COUNTRY

He went back to his hands. Back to his studio where he always worked with his hands. He worked on himself without looking down at it, without versatility, as relentlessly as the time the dentist's novocaine had settled into his chin: He was in the car, waiting, his mother in a store, the lower half of his face feelingless gristle. But far under the thick surface there was an itch at the center, and he scratched and rubbed, gnawed with his fingernails, crying, I can't get to it, Mom. When the novocaine wore off, they discovered he'd scraped the skin off his jaw.

Morning. Movement in the outer rooms. The others were coming home to eat breakfast and go to work. Or, like Marsha, to sleep a while before starting over. Phelan wiped his hands on the sheets of his unmade bed. He left the sheets balled-up and sticky. In a few hours they were dry and crusty. He didn't strip the bed and change the linen.

He sat there and listened to bowls rattle and water run. He heard Anna laugh. After a while he heard Robyn grumble in the kitchen on the other side of his studio wall. Doors banged, dishes dropped in the sink, water turned off, footsteps thumped, the front door hinge sang. Keys turned in the lock. The house was empty. Late morning. Phelan got off his bed.

He looked into the kitchen. Cereal bowls in the sink. A frying pan on the stove, grease turning white. A fly walking on the thin edge of an open milk carton on the shelf. He tied his bathrobe around his waist. Anna had made the robe and given it to him for his birthday when he turned twenty-five. Now he was twenty-five and a half.

He took a handful of potato chips from someone's cupboard and went into the living room. He crunched the chips one at a time then wiped his fingers on the arm of the couch. The phone rang; he stared at it. Then it stopped.

There were several pairs of shoes in the living room, and a man's smelly shirt was carelessly slung over the back of the couch. Someone had put a damp towel over the only lamp, but the lamp wasn't turned on. A cockroach walked along the edge of Anna's ashtray, which had been empty last night but now was full. The cockroach didn't go down into the bowl of the ashtray. There was another ashtray with a brown banana peel in it. The phone rang again. Phelan went back into his studio.

The morning-lit windows and fire-colored curtains tinted his room. His books. His tools. His bed. Everything motionless. Waiting. Dust was thick, floating in the sunlight. He batted at it with slow, swimming movements, but he trembled and his breath became short like that night he drove home through a coastal fog in California, every window flat black, the head-lights unable to penetrate. People on the coast called it "socked in," and he was alone in it, inching forward, or perhaps not moving at all, there was no way to tell, and no one else to see, white darkness. His fists gripping the wheel, his legs jerking irrationally, an adrenalin rush so violent his stomach burned, he lost his breath, he shouted, then breathed again, panting, fogging the windows from the inside as well. "I was so desperate to get out," he'd told Anna, "I would've done *anything* to get home, swim along the coast, jump from tree to tree, even slither along on my stomach in the only clear place—six inches off the ground." But finally, like driving off a cliff, the fog ended abruptly, and he could see the stars and the streetlights again.

He'd never previously considered dust in sunlight to be even remotely the same. Every time he passed his hand through, thousands more swam in to fill the space, so hazy he could hardly see the wall, his workbench, the bed, the things he'd bought, carefully chosen, pictures, lamps, decorations, his project—all behind a haze of dust, fading. With both hands he swam faster, stirring it up, but it settled on books and furniture, on top of the layers of dust already there, and under the bed—balls of dust. The world was inverted and clouds sat on the floor. Everything buried, crumbling, ruins of an ancient civilization. His hands were fists, his lips drawn back, he turned abruptly toward his project, his voice heavy but barely audible, "You!" Just one blow, the clay thing took it in the gut and doubled, a sculpture of a fist-print.

With his hands in the pockets of his bathrobe, he returned to the kitchen. Marsha was at the sink, filling a glass with water. She took two pills.

"Hi Phelan."

"Hi."

"How's everything been going for you?"

"Okay."

"I haven't seen you for a while."

"I guess not."

"How's everything at school?"

"Fine."

"I have one student," she said. "How many do you have?"

"Five."

"Don't you have a class today?"

"Yes."

"Oh," she smiled. "Everyone needs a break now and then."

"Yes," he said. He looked at her. No laughter hiding in her eyes. Only the tranquil smile, and suddenly but smoothly, she reached out and put her hand on his arm.

"Anyway, the classroom's always open," he said. "They can work on their projects. As if any amount of work will do any good."

"Your students aren't talented?"

"I don't know, but all I can teach is technique. They're all discouraged and I can't do anything about that."

He felt her hand tighten slightly on his arm. He went on: "I mean, a teacher can't teach them to give up, but —"

"Take it easy. Don't feel responsible."

"I was paid to teach art —" He paused, taking several quick breaths. "Fucking art schools — what the hell good does it do anyone! Pointless bullshit —"

"Phelan . . ." She slid her hand down his arm and took his hand, which was a fist. She loosened his fingers. "Anyone can go stale, it's perfectly normal." She looked down at his hand. "I'm sorry, Phelan. You seemed so happy, and . . . well, really, I *am* sorry. . . ."

He stared at the top of her head until she looked up.

"Maybe it was for the best, anyway," she said, smiling again. He opened his mouth but didn't say anything. As she held his hand, she rubbed the back of it with her thumb.

"I mean, it wasn't really what you wanted anyway, was it?"

He set his lips. "What the hell difference does that make?"

"Don't say that!" She released his hand and held his face with her thumb and forefinger, pinching his cheeks together, shaking him, laughing, for a second. Then she stepped back, suddenly calm. "But really, Phelan, I understand, I really do — and you really are the only person in this house, in this whole damn city, who I respect."

He rolled his eyes and laughed, a short, single sound.

"Hey!" She reached out and pushed him a little, with her fingertips. "Don't laugh, it's my honest opinion."

"No, I didn't mean you. It's me — look at me: not dressed, not working, ditching my job, a veritable pillar of society — "

"*Stop it!*"

He did stop, and he looked at her. They looked at each other. He pulled on his lip with one hand, then let it snap back.

"I'm thinking about maybe going home for a while," he said. He put his hands into the pockets of his robe.

"Home as in *home?*"

"California."

"You don't want to do that," she said. Then, "You know how?"

He blinked a few times. "Get on a plane."

Marsha laughed and she explained the paperwork for leaving the country. She suggested he change his money on the black market. The *cambios,* she said, were solely in the business of exchanging money. And you got a better rate the farther down the street you went. Cops guarded the black market, which meant it was sort of legal but not so legal, which was how someone at the bank once explained it to her.

"Oh," Phelan said.

"But you don't want to do that . . . go home, I mean."

"Why not?"

She smiled and touched his arm again, but just briefly. "Because you don't want to teach your students to give up."

He moved like slow motion and put his fist through the window. No — the window shattered by itself. No — the window was still whole. A ringing in his ears broke. And sweat broke. Only his voice didn't break. "But how can a person be taught to *not* get disappointed?"

"Now *there's* a question," she said.

His hands in his pockets had loosened his robe in front, although it was still tied with the cord, so the edges of the robe had separated a little. His penis showed.

"Really, though, Phelan, if you're looking for what you're bound to get, how can you be disappointed?"

She smiled at him. He didn't fix his robe. They looked at each other for a while. He heard a stereo in the apartment overhead, suddenly aware of the thumping rhythm, over and over. Finally he said, "Is that it?" but neither of them moved, looking at each other, until in a single motion he stepped aside and she moved past him out of the kitchen.

Marsha shut the door. He looked briefly at his feet. He wore the kind of slippers old men wear.

He didn't move. She came up close to him, lifted the collar of his robe and kissed his neck. She held the two front edges of his robe, pulling them farther apart as she kissed down his chest to his stomach. Then she straightened again and untied the cord, slowly opened his robe all the way, peeled it back over his shoulders, lowered it and dropped it in a ring around his feet.

"Oh, Phelan," she grinned, "you've a magnificent tool."

He laughed harshly and came toward her, backing her up to the bed. She shrieked, falling down on the mattress, covering her face with her hands. He followed, falling forward, falling onto her. "Wait, wait, wait," she said from underneath. He just lay there. She pushed him aside a little and sat up. "It's okay, Phelan, but save it for a sec. I don't want to rip my clothes." She shed her clothing quickly, dropping it all over the edge of the bed. "Okay, you got me undressed," she giggled. "See how much farther you can get!" He lay beside her. "Try to get on top," she said. He rolled onto her, but her hands against his chest pushed him back. He almost fell off the bed. "Try harder!" she urged. She began to breathe heavily. He pinned both of her wrists to the mattress, one in each of his hands, but she coiled her legs and braced her feet on his stomach. When he released her arms to push her legs aside, her hands were back against his body, holding him off. Her skinny arms had hard muscles. "Try," she gasped. Then she rolled toward the wall, pressing her legs together and tightening her flat rump. He grabbed her arm, but she kept slipping away, slapping at him, so he held her waist and jerked her to her back, mounting her, but her knee was up, her arms holding him back, "Try, try," she laughed, her arms rigid, her knee braced between them. "Try harder," she said. He threw himself at her again, their bones bumped together, he bruised his hips against her, their ribs rubbed each other. She got a knee between their bodies and again pushed him back, again holding him there with legs straight and both feet against his chest. "Come on," she said hoarsely. He grabbed her ankles and ripped her legs apart. She laughed hysterically. He touched her with just the tip of his penis before she pulled her legs up again and kicked him back, laughing, "No! No!" She opened her eyes. Her arms didn't weaken. He lifted his fist. She continued to laugh, looking up at him.

# 32

## WORKING AT HOME

I'm going to get a mirror and see what's going on down here. You must have one somewhere, put away in a drawer or in that box of stuff you won't unpack but won't throw away.

Here it is—chipped, but it'll work.

Prop it up with the pillow at the foot of the bed, and I'll be able to see what I'm doing.

But the angle's wrong and I can only see the ceiling. Yet even as I tip and adjust the mirror with my feet, I've only got a moving picture, like from a train window, of the headboard, lamp, clock, books. . . .

What's wrong with this thing!

What if I put the mirror on an easel and stood in front—what would I see?

Who painted all my paintings?

Holding me down, holding me still. "My best story ever. Because it takes place right here, with us. Listen!"

*No!*

I *wouldn't* hear it. That's why: The best story ended before the title. Paints and easel and everything flying through the air.

Paints, canvas, brushes, jars of water, coffee cups, empty plates. . . .

*How the hell could I miss!*

*I* was the one spattered and streaked. Colors dripping down my neck. I was the one tattooed, rainbowed, sprayed with color. You said I was beautiful. Hugged me, getting the same colors all over you. And you finger-painted.

The whole time you were bathing me, I wanted to kill something.

# 33

## HOW TO LEAVE A COUNTRY

It was January, but summer in Brazil. He took a bus to the university. It took an hour as usual. He got a green chip and threw it out the window. He resigned his teaching position then took a bus back to the apartment, and that took an hour and a half.

Back in his studio: pans of brown water, muddy towels, dirty tools. The clay thing still stood under a soiled wet cloth. He stuffed it into a pillow case and tied the top like a laundry bag.

He used the robe Anna had made for him to wipe up spilled muddy water and clay fragments on the workbench and the floor. He dropped the tools into their box, still dirty, uncounted.

All of his clothes were dirty. He left them on the floor of the closet. He stripped the bed so quickly, the sheets ripped. He threw them in the closet also. The mattress he stood against the wall, over the windows. Lamps, books, decorations, pictures were stacked together. Several things broke as he tossed them into the corner. He dismantled the workbench and bookcase and leaned the lumber against one of the empty walls. He removed all the nails and threw them into the corner with the books and pictures. A few more things broke when hit by the nails.

He looked around the room. One more picture on the wall. Anna's painting of flowers. He lifted it from the nail and sat down in the armchair — still in the middle of the room. He'd never noticed how the light sprinklings of sand and salt in the paint sparkled just a little in the flowers, and if he rocked the canvas back and forth, side to side, slowly, gently, they looked like real flowers, freshly sprayed with water, perhaps a breeze blowing over them — especially if he also squinted at the same time. But then he noticed all the thumbprints around the edge of the canvas, blue or black, and the bunch of flowers clashed with pink, purple, red, turquoise, even green — a light *green* flower! And the stems fat, uneven, no leaves, no end — the stems went clear to the edge of the canvas and stopped there. He picked up a nail and scraped as much paint off the canvas as possible. It took a long time, but he didn't know where his razor blades would be in the mess. The nail went through the canvas a couple of times. There was always a shadow of the picture still there. He stopped scraping and poked the nail in and out until he couldn't find a place big enough to push it through one more time. He flung the canvas onto the pile of things and sat in the chair a while more, digging under his fingernails with the point of the nail. He drew blood a few times.

He went outside and picked all the letters off the marquee. He didn't know where the letters of his name were. He went back to the room and pawed around for them in the pile of stuff, then he abruptly whirled and threw all the other letters against a wall and let them lie where they fell.

When Anna came in, he was sitting on the floor, the clay between his legs, the pillow case peeled down the sides of it.

He had a tool in one hand. He was poking it into the clay. It wasn't a knife. It was looped metal and didn't make clean holes. The clay ripped, pieces came out when he withdrew the tool, dropping around him like mud.

Anna knocked and opened the door. "I knew you were home. . . ."

His arm with the tool paused, just for a second, then continued, faster. She stepped closer, mashing bits of clay under her feet. "I have the mail."

"I don't want it."

"Well . . . it's a few bills."

He heard her open her purse. Then she began walking around the room. He stopped to watch her. She kicked some stuff aside and opened a drawer, lifted a few things and found his checkbook. "Maybe if I make out a check for your share, you can sign it. . . ."

He turned back to the clay, poking the tool in, twisting it, pulling out. Bigger pieces fell on the floor.

"Here . . ." She stood beside him, holding out a check.

"My hands are dirty."

"Phelan. . ."

"You go ahead and sign it — it'll be just as good."

She kneeled beside him, brushed bits of clay aside, put the check on the floor and signed his name. His tool shoveled clay fragments into her hair and onto her legs.

"What're you doing?"

"What difference does it make?"

"I thought you might want to talk about it."

He didn't answer.

"I mean . . . I *told* you. . . ."

He shut his eyes but didn't stop his arm.

"And I wasn't going to let myself be disappointed by expecting whatever it was you were planning to actually *happen.*"

There was only the soft, gritty sound of the tool hitting the clay. Then Anna's voice again, "Don't think you're punishing me, Phelan. I don't feel guilty. Nothing was happening so I had to do something for myself. I'm sorry if I upset your plans."

His arm froze, pointing the tool at her. "You think it's just because of *you? Bullshit!*"

She was standing. She went to the door. He resumed his task, cocking his arm over his head, plunging the tool into the clay, ripping it out, his arm flying up, cocking over his head. . . .

Anna in the doorway, "What the hell do you want from everyone anyway, Phelan?"

He didn't look at her again. She left.

In a moment he threw the tool across the room.

Next he masturbated. He found an old hand mirror of Anna's with only one crack across it. He sat in the chair and propped the mirror up to watch himself. He rubbed in silence. A silent film of a man scraping a carrot. When the noise came, it sounded like laughter.

A knock on the door and Cassie said, "Phelan, I'm home. Did you pick up my mail?"

"Just a sec. I'm jacking off."

"What?" She opened the door and came in.

He didn't stop. "What do you want?"

"I don't know. What're you doing?"

"I don't know."


He grabbed her. Tried to screw her. Tried to pin her down like a bug writhing on a specimen tray.

She grabbed him too. Held him like a knife handle. He wasn't sure which way the blade would be pointing. He didn't care.

He growled.

She giggled.

He bit. All over. Even himself.

She kept moving around, changing positions.

He didn't stay hard.

She tried to pump it up. She tugged and twisted. It didn't work.

He slapped her.

She slapped back, so he hit her again.

175

She was crying. "Please . . ." She tugged weakly on his penis. He brought her hand to his mouth to bite her.

She grabbed his hair in a fistful.

He knocked her away, caught her legs so she fell on the floor, he landed on top. Her body was spongy. She scratched him. He put one hand over her mouth and kept pounding the floor beside her head with his other fist.

He was bleeding from the mouth where he'd bitten his own tongue and lips.

She huddled behind the chair and fucked herself. Used her fingers. Used both hands. "I can't help it," she sobbed. Phelan watched. Sprawled on the floor. Limbs in four directions.

He went immediately to the bank and closed his account, took the cash to the black market, exchanged it, then went out and bought new clothes, using the checks from his closed account — they had neglected to take the checks away from him. He bought each article of clothing in a different store, writing ten checks in all. He also bought a suitcase.

Because he was a permanent resident, they said, he wouldn't be able to buy a ticket to leave Brazil (to any country) unless he first paid a deposit of $1,000, which he did not have. So he applied for an exemption. They asked if he was going abroad to study. He said no. They asked if he had an important job in another country. He said no. They rejected his application to leave because he couldn't convince them that he would accomplish anything for the greater glory of Brazil.

He applied again at another office and lied. They said his application would take at least a month to process.

He went to the *despechante*. The lawyer picked up the five dollar bill Phelan put down, and said he was sorry it was taking so long, but the ID card should be ready soon, very soon. The wheels were finally greased and turning.

Phelan put down another five dollar bill; the *despechante* picked it up. "Forget the wheels," Phelan said. He put down a ten dollar bill. "Fix my papers so I've never been here."

The *despechante* didn't pick up the ten dollars. He leaned back. His chair squeaked. Phelan signed a check and tore it out of the book.

He was the only one who walked through the turnstile and onto the jet. There was no one asking him for a ticket, checking his passport and baggage, assigning him a seat, offering him headphones or a meal, saying excuse-me-is-this-seat-taken. He closed his eyes.

The arrival was never announced, nor the temperature, the weather, the time of day. It was someplace he'd never been. When he got home, she was already there, lying on some pillows in the living room — on her stomach, knees bent, ankles hooked together in the air over her back. A lamp on the floor. Beneath it, beside her, a cat, stretched on its side, slowly lifting and curling its tail, then uncoiling it to softly thump the floor. And in front of her, a chess game.

The room was warm. He stripped to his underwear. And the room was silent — no clock ticking. But the cat purred.

Together, he and she looked down at the chess game on the floor between them. She made a move and he answered it, sweeping the pieces aside and pulling her close. They held one another, fitting together, looking at each other's muddy orphan faces. . . .

*No, Tara, don't ask. Stop — Wait — Everything will stay the same as long as you never know how I made your perfect life —*

# 34

## LION HUNTING

*Did you expect something more spectacular?*

There's no breeze. A mockingbird in one of the pines begins to call. First it sounds like a meadowlark, then a sparrow. The only call it can't reproduce is that of the mourning doves.

Even after he'd stopped coming up here for other reasons, he'd brought his chess set to this spot, his oldest set, the one he'd found in his grandfather's garage. At first he just set up complex positions and studied them. As the sun moved and the shadows of the chess pieces changed angles, he saw more variations. Hours of analysis, investigation, meditation, contemplation, lying on his stomach as still as lizards lay in the sun, not feeling his own hunger nor the ache in his neck and shoulders. Then he would abruptly flex a leg and kick the ground, snatch up the pieces and set up a new position. The lizards on the rocks ran and hid, but their fear soon forgotten, came out again to doze as long as there was sunlight, until the next time Phelan's study failed to lead him to an answer.

Daybreak is calm. He's looking at the empty board drawn in the sand, seeing combinations, positions and possibilities, even without pieces to maneuver. Ant lions have begun building their homes for the day — smooth funnels of fine sand appear on the board and around the edges.

Chess study was a one-man game. A few times he had brought his stepmother's old chipped hand mirror up here and planted it in the sand on the other side of the chessboard. Different than any real game he'd ever played. Usually both players are intent on the board — if either looked up he would only see the top of the other's head. But those times up here he'd found himself staring across the board into the mirror, trying to figure out what his opponent was thinking, and the mirror stared back, wondering the same, until both laughed with relief — not because they found their answers, but because they remembered that good strategy never includes hoping the other guy will make a mistake you can take advantage of.

*What would Tara have said if she'd ever seen me up here with the mirror?*

*She would've automatically understood . . . wouldn't she? Wouldn't she?*

*I can't go back there.*

*I wonder if she threw the cat out into the weeds like she wanted to, to see if he knew of another way to live. If I'd brought him with me, I could've followed him, gone with him, but . . . it's been several hours, I don't remember if he was real either. . . .*

The ant lion colony grows, eroding away the outline of the chessboard. Phelan laughs, lies down, his head on his arm, laughing.

The English coffee house of the 1600s
was a place of fellowship where
ideas were freely exchanged.

The Parisian cafes of the early 1900s
witnessed the birth of dadaism,
cubism and surrealism.

The American coffee house of the 1950s,
a refuge from conformity for beat poets,
exploded with literary energy.

This spirit lives on in the pages
of Coffee House Press books.

*How To Leave a Country* was designed by Allan Kornblum using the Xerox Ventura desktop publishing system. The Sabon type was generated by Stanton Publication Services. Coffee House Press books are printed on acid-free paper and have sewn bindings for durability.